ONE GOOD TURN . . .

Fiona will do anything for her best friend, even looking after her trouble-some dog, Archie. When Archie pulls yet another stunt, this time raiding a picnic at the park, she and Archie are rescued by handsome Tom and his impeccably trained dog, Dixon. When Tom offers to help with Archie's train-ing, Fiona can't refuse and finds herself falling in love. But Tom has secrets which threaten their relationship. Can Fiona learn to trust again or risk losing her happy ever after?

SARAH PURDUE

ONE GOOD TURN . . .

Complete and Unabridged

LINFORD
Leicester

First published in Great Britain in 2019

First Linford Edition
published 2020

A catalogue record for this book is available
from the British Library.

ISBN 978–1–4448–4635–5

Published by
Ulverscroft Limited
Anstey, Leicestershire

Set by Words & Graphics Ltd.
Anstey, Leicestershire
Printed and bound in Great Britain by
TJ Books Limited, Padstow, Cornwall

This book is printed on acid-free paper

Dogged by Disaster

'No, no, no!' Fiona whispered to herself. 'Not again.' She tried to plaster what she hoped was a confident smile across her face and ran across the stretch of grass. She held her hands up in what she hoped would be interpreted as the universal sign of an apology as she approached the French tourists and what was left of their picnic.

Fiona racked her brains for any remembrance of high school French but with no luck, she went for English.

'I am so sorry. He's not my dog and he managed to get off his lead.'

The French matriarch stared at Fiona and then back to the carefully laid out picnic blanket, which now had a trail of muddy paw-prints and significantly less food than it had started with.

The woman nodded as she threw a

comforting arm around her small son. He was pointing in the direction that Archie had run off in, but all that could be seen was a small fluffy behind and the boy's baguette, which Archie was holding upright like a flag.

Fiona felt in her pocket for her purse. Opening it, she realised she had hardly any cash. Who carried cash these days, she asked herself in dismay.

Fiona emptied the odd collection of coins out into her hand and offered them to the French woman, all the while trying to keep an eye on the direction that Archie was heading. No doubt he was looking for a suitable spot to devour his spoils.

The French lady stared at the small collection of coins and shook her head, seemingly in disbelief.

'I'm so sorry — I didn't bring any other money out with me.'

Fiona couldn't tell if her words were being understood or not but decided that her presence only seemed to be making things worse, not to mention that a small crowd appeared to be forming and some of them held up their mobile phones to film her embarrassment.

'OK, I'll just leave it here,' Fiona said as she gingerly laid the coins down on the crumpled, muddy edge of the blanket. 'And once again, I am so, so sorry.' Fiona started backing away, as the woman and her child simply stared at her.

She tried one last smile and then started running in the last known direction of Archibald the Terrible, the new name that Fiona had given the blighter since she had offered to look after him only three days before.

Three days! Fiona thought. How could such a small dog cause such chaos in such a short period of time?

Becky had been desperate. Her usual dog sitter had let her down at the last moment and Archie apparently hadn't done well in kennels the last time he had been there.

That, thought Fiona, should have

been her first clue. She had a deep suspicion now that it had more to do with how well the kennels had coped with Archie rather than the other way round.

An image of Becky's face swam into view. There was no doubt about it. Becky loved Archie and he had got her through some deep personal heartache, and now Becky's dad was unwell. Fiona ran faster. One thing was for sure — she wasn't going to lose Archie, however embarrassed she might feel by his behaviour. There was no way she was going to tell Becky that she had lost him.

No, she was going to find the terror, give him a proper telling off and then take him back home, where at least the damage could be confined to her tiny flat.

After ten minutes of running, the embarrassment and crossness had been replaced by fear. Fiona kept running and calling and was feeling more and more desperate. There were people everywhere, some had dogs, some didn't, but there was no sign of Archie.

She stopped and asked a few people if they had seen him but the people only shook their heads and gave her looks of sympathy. Out of breath and feeling on the verge of tears, she stopped and shouted his name.

'Archie! Archie?'

She knew it was pointless. He never came when she called. He was the most stubborn and wilful animal she had ever met. Please, she said silently, please come back.

Fiona turned around slowly, scanning for any signs of him or any signs of the mayhem that he usually left in his wake but there was nothing.

'Excuse me?' a voice said behind her, making her jump just a little.

'Yes?' she said distractedly, turning around to see the source of the voice.

'I think I may have found what you are looking for.'

At that moment, Fiona felt the all too familiar scrabbling at her jeans, leaving trails of mud and what looked like mayonnaise from the offending baguette.

'Archie!' Fiona shouted. She knelt down and Archie threw himself into her arms. For a moment Fiona forgot all the stress he had caused and was overwhelmed with a sense of relief. She stood up, keeping a firm hold on Archie and noticed his rescuer for the first time.

It has his eyes Fiona noticed first. Bright blue and seemingly giving out a light of their own. He was taller than Fiona and so she had to look up to see him properly.

He had closely cropped hair and he was wearing a faintly amused kind of smile. Fiona realised that Archie was still attached to the man by way of a lead.

'Thank you so much,' she said, her voice coming out breathless and she felt embarrassment burn inside her. 'I can't believe you had a lead with you.'

The man raised an eyebrow and looked down. Fiona followed his gaze and took in the silky black spaniel who was sitting quietly beside him, looking up attentively in a way that Archie had never done. This man was clearly in charge and Fiona felt the need to explain.

'Archie's not my dog,' Fiona said, feeling a little flash of guilt at laying the blame at Becky's door. 'I'm just looking after him for a friend and so I don't really know what I'm doing.'

The man nodded and Fiona had to look away. She was making it worse and she needed to stop talking.

'I see,' the man said and there was more amusement showing on his face. 'Well, I had to smooth things over with a couple having a picnic, he stormed their blanket and ran off with a Scotch egg.'

Fiona's eyes went wide.

'Did he?' she asked, thinking that this day could only get worse.

'Don't worry, I sorted it out but you probably need to get him under control. Not everyone will laugh it off.'

The man's face turned serious.

Fiona knew that he was probably right. She had been lucky so far but not everyone would either be too stunned to say anything or able to laugh it off.

'I don't know where to start,' she said, looking down at Archie who had rolled over in her arms as if butter wouldn't melt. She started realising that she had said the words out loud.

'I'm sorry, what I should be saying is thank you. Archie's owner is having a really hard time at the moment and I promised I would look after him. I can't . . . ' She felt the words catch in her throat at the thought of having to give Becky more bad news. She shook herself. She needed to get a grip. Archie was fine. All she needed to do was get him home.

'Hey,' the man said and Fiona felt him rest a gentle hand on her shoulder. 'Don't beat yourself up. Not many people would do what you've done. And it's not your fault that he slipped his lead or that he has to learn proper manners.'

Fiona smiled. At least someone was giving an honest assessment of Archie.

'He's obviously a handful,' the man added.

Fiona nodded, not really trusting herself to say anything.

'How much longer have you got him for?'

'Not sure, really. My friend has gone to Sheffield to look after her dad who's poorly.'

'Then why don't you let me give you a few lessons?'

Fiona blinked. She was expecting him to make his excuses and leave but here he was offering to help her. But she had only just met this man — should she trust him?

'I train dogs for a living,' he told her and the look on his face told Fiona that he knew exactly what she was thinking.

'I'm sorry, I didn't mean any-thing . . . ' Her voice trailed away, she was making it worse again.

'No you're right to be cautious. You've only just met me, but what I was going to suggest was that we meet here at the park. There will be lots of people about so you won't need to worry.'

He looked serious, not as if he was teasing her, and he waited.

'That is really kind of you, but I can't ask you to do that.'

Now he smiled, gently and reassuringly and Fiona felt her heart leap just a little.

'It's no trouble. I bring Dixon down most evenings, around six. Archie will probably learn best if Dixon can show him the basics.'

Fiona nodded. It was tempting. After all, she really did have no idea how long Becky would be away and it wasn't as though keeping Archie indoors was an option. More than that, she didn't think she could face another walk like she had just had.

'Well, if you're sure you don't mind?'

'I don't mind,' he said, smiling. 'Why don't we swap mobile numbers?'

Fiona smiled and nodded. She wasn't in the habit of giving out her phone number to people she had just met, even apparently nice friendly guys. This was London, after all. But he did seem genuine and it wasn't as if she was giving him her home address.

'Sure,' Fiona said. 'We should probably know each other's names as well.'

The man nodded but waited for Fiona to go first.

'I'm Fiona.'

'Tom.' And there was that smile again. Just the right kind of smile, Fiona thought, a little dreamily. Not over the top, not flirty — just friendly and kind.

Tom pulled a small notebook from inside his jacket pocket and wrote down his phone number. Fiona was impressed that he was so organised. She was lucky if she remembered her keys and her phone when she left the house.

He handed over the piece of paper and Fiona wondered how she was going to write down her own without letting go of Archie.

'I can write it down,' Tom suggested and once more Fiona felt like he was reading her mind. She nodded and told him her address.

'Well, Dixon and I will be here tomorrow and Tuesday night if you fancy joining us.'

'I will. Thank you for capturing him and everything.'

'Take the lead. It's better than the one you have and should mean you get home safely.'

'I'll get one like it and bring yours back,' Fiona said, feeling like this was all rather one sided, with Tom doing so much for her and she not being able to return the favour.

'No problem, we have several at home.'

'Do you want to take mine, to get Dixon home?'

They both looked down. Dixon had remained in the same spot and showed no sign of running away.

'I think we'll be fine, thanks,' Tom said with a smile.

'He's amazing,' Fiona said, thinking that looking after Dixon would be so much easier than Archie. And looking at Tom, she suspected that Dixon didn't wake him up every hour as Archie had been doing to her since he arrived.

'Archie's got it in him, you'll see,' Tom said with a confidence that Fiona didn't feel. 'We'll be here tomorrow at six, if you want to join us, but no pressure.'

Fiona looked down at Archie in her arms and then back at to Tom.

'We'll be here,' Fiona said quickly as she tried to ignore the feeling that it wasn't just about getting Archie trained.

'See you tomorrow, then,' Tom said with a wave before he started striding off in the other direction with Dixon at his heels.

Archie licked Fiona's nose and made some snuffling noises that sounded like he was laughing.

'And you can stop that. I'm only

meeting up with him again to get you trained.'

If dogs could raise an eyebrow then Fiona was sure that Archie was doing just that. With a firm grip on the lead, she put him down.

'And yes, the fact that he seems lovely has nothing to do with it,' she whispered to Archie, not believing a word of it herself.

Help is at Hand

Working from home had many advantages, Fiona had always thought. She did have to go to meetings sometimes, but on the whole she was based at home. It meant she could set her own hours, didn't have to deal with the daily struggle of commuting to work and could, if she chose to, stay in her pyjamas all day.

It also meant she was the only person who could have possibly dog sat Archie.

It was ten minutes to five in the morning. Archie was lying lengthways across the bed, legs in the air and snoring loudly enough to bother the neighbours. Fiona, on the other hand, was awake, and as hard as she tried she could not get back to sleep.

Archie had been wide awake until about twenty minutes ago and judging by his current status, now intended to sleep for the rest of the day — a luxury that Fiona could not afford. All she could do was hope that some training with Tom might make him a little more manageable.

With a sigh she got up. She might as well get on with some work, then maybe she could have a lie down later, before she went out to meet Tom.

Fiona was yawning as she led Archie to the park on his new lead. Tom had been right and, so far, Archie hadn't been able to do his usual trick and slip out of it. In fact he was trotting along beside her quite calmly. He looked annoyingly refreshed.

Fiona had not been able to squeeze in a nap. Work had been busy and some of her customers unusually demanding. She fought another yawn as her mind turned to the thought of meeting up with Tom again.

That thought had been an added distraction to her day but at least it had been a happy thought. In fact she felt like she was going on a first date, which she knew that she wasn't but still . . . London could be a lonely place and it wasn't just Archie who was missing Becky. It would be nice to have some company for a little while, that wasn't canine.

Fiona caught sight of Tom, standing a little way away from the coffee shop with Dixon waiting patiently at his side.

Tom's tall outline was unmistakable. He was wearing jeans and boots, with a checked shirt and jacket. On anyone else it might have looked like he was going for the lumberjack look but on Tom it just looked natural — not to mention handsome.

When Tom looked in her direction, Fiona held up a hand in a wave and hoped that she was far enough away to avoid Tom's seeming ability to read her mind.

Tom waved back and smiled and then his smile suddenly dropped. He shouted something that Fiona could not hear and then a splash of water caught her attention. A millisecond later she felt the cold water drench her legs. At the same time she realised that Archie's lead had gone slack in her hand.

Tom was by her side and Dixon seemed to be looking at her with curiosity, as if he was trying to work out how she had let Archie do what he had just done. Fiona was thinking the same thing. Archie, having completed his dive bomb move, was now swimming steadily across the lake.

'You're soaked,' Tom said with concern.

'I don't know how he did it,' she said.

'He is a master of escape,' Tom said, taking his eyes from his inspection of Fiona to the sight of Archie swimming across the lake to the island at its centre.

'Here!' an angry voice said. 'No dogs in the lake! What's the matter with you? Can't you read the signs?'

Fiona expected to see some sort of park ranger in a uniform but instead

18

she was confronted by an older, well-dressed man who was brandishing his walking stick.

'Your dog is scaring the birds and some of them are protected species.'

'I'm so sorry,' Fiona managed to say.

'The dog slipped his lead. It was an accident and we will get him back,' Tom said coolly, clearly unfazed by the man's anger, which Fiona thought was probably justified.

Archie meanwhile was steadily making his way across the lake and getting closer and closer to the island in the middle.

'Archie!' Fiona shouted. Archie naturally ignored her or perhaps he had water in his ears and had gone suddenly deaf. Fiona couldn't be sure.

'He'll never come back,' Fiona said, turning her attention from the angry man, who had his hands on his hips and was tutting loudly, to Tom.

Tom lifted his fingers to his lips and let out an ear piercing whistle. Dixon at his side seemed to be ready to leap in to action, should action be required. Fiona looked out to where Archie was and could see that he had at least stopped and was now sort of treading water.

Tom's eyes were focused on Archie and Fiona wondered if he knew some kind of mind trick that allowed him to communicate with dogs without actually using any words.

Fiona opened her mouth to call Archie's name. Perhaps he would come back to her now? But Tom reached out a hand for her arm and she kept silent. All of Tom's focus was on the doggy-paddling pooch.

There seemed to be some kind of staring competition going on and then Tom whistled again, low and long. Archie seemed to have fallen under Tom's spell because at that moment he turned around and started making his way back to the bank.

Archie reached the water's edge and Tom grabbed him by the collar, just in case he decided to change his mind. Tom took the lead from Fiona's hand and reattached it to Archie, who sat next to Dixon, looking as if he couldn't understand what all the fuss was about.

'Just see that you keep that dog under better control,' the older man said before he stalked off. Fiona watched him going, feeling as if she was going to cry. She was doing her best, but it didn't seem to matter what she tried to do, Archie was a magnet for trouble.

'Let's get you home. It's too cold to be standing around in wet clothes,' Tom said as he carefully held Archie's lead at arm's length as the dog shook off some of the lake water.

Fiona's earlier caution about not revealing too much of herself to Tom had been thrown to the wind. Surely he had done enough to prove to her that she could trust him to know where she lived. Fiona reached out a hand for Archie's lead.

'I think it's best if I keep hold of him,' Tom said. His eyes were serious but he offered up a small smile and Fiona managed one back.

Tom set them off at quite a pace and

when they reached the edge of the park he waited for Fiona to lead the way.

'I could call us a taxi,' he said looking at her with concern.

'It will be quicker to walk,' Fiona said, trying to keep her voice steady and her teeth from chattering.

It took them less than ten minutes to reach the front door to the old Victorian house where Fiona lived. She had the ground floor which meant she also had access to the small back garden.

She didn't think she could live in London without some outside space, even with the park so close. It had cost her a premium but she was happy to skimp on other areas of her life to have the garden.

When Fiona had unlocked the front door, Tom handed her Archie's lead.

'Go and get warmed up. How about we try again tomorrow, if you want?'

'Come in. The least I can do is get you a hot drink.' Fiona smiled at him. Tom looked back at her levelly and she felt sure he was checking that she really did want to ask him in and not that she felt obliged.

'If you're sure?' Tom asked.

'Of course, and I'm sure I can find Dixon a dog biscuit and a bowl of water.'

Dixon's ears seemed to prick up at the word dog 'biscuit' and Tom laughed.

'In that case how could we refuse?'

Fiona led the way across the hall, as Tom closed the front door behind them. Fiona kept hold of Archie in case he decided to go and explore upstairs, which he had done before, causing some grumbling from her upstairs neighbours.

Once inside Fiona let go of the lead and Archie ran for the sofa and proceeded to use the cover to dry himself off.

Fiona winced, but at least she had remembered to cover the material with an old throw that she could then chuck in the washing machine.

'I see that his manners aren't any

better at home,' Tom said.

Fiona looked at him sharply, wondering if it was a criticism, which she didn't think she could take any more of but Tom was shaking his head and smiling. Fiona relaxed.

'I'll put the kettle on and go and change,' she said, heading towards the bedroom.

Once she had swapped her wet jeans for her fleecy jogging bottoms, Fiona felt better. She headed back out to the lounge and found Tom standing at the patio doors looking out to the garden.

'Your garden is beautiful,' Tom said, sounding a little in awe.

Fiona took in the narrow garden with the century old oak tree at the end, casting shadows in the autumn light. The garden had been loved before she arrived and so Fiona couldn't take credit for the layout.

Climbers grew up the walls which surrounded it and the beds still had some colour despite the fact that it was October. Between the walls and the tree it was possible to imagine that you were somewhere other than London.

'It's the reason I bought the flat,' Fiona said softly, not wanting to break the spell. 'I couldn't imagine living in London without a little outside space, even with the park so near.'

The flat itself was tiny. Her bedroom fitted a double bed and not much else. The rest of the flat, bar the tiny bathroom that was only big enough for a shower and a toilet, fitted into one room but Fiona loved it all the same.

'I have to admit to being a little jealous,' Tom said, not being able to pull his eyes away from the garden as Fiona used some of her secret stash of posh hot chocolate that she kept for emergencies.

'It's not easy to find a place that's affordable and this place is a stretch. I inherited some money from my grandad for the deposit and well, let's just say I don't go out much to spend any money.'

'I think it's worth it,' Tom said, taking

the proffered mug and cradling it in his hands. 'I need to be near work and the kennels so I didn't have too much choice on location.'

Fiona nodded, although she wondered why a dog trainer needed to live close to work but shrugged it off. Who was she to question other people's choices? Hers had certainly been questioned by friends and family.

She walked over to the sofa and Archie looked up at her and she pointed to his bed. It was a very expensive memory foam dog bed but yet Archie still preferred to sleep anywhere else. Fiona raised an eyebrow and, with a grumble, Archie trotted over to his bed. Dixon of course was curled up next to it, like any well behaved dog might do.

Fiona pulled off the now mud-stained cover and indicated that Tom should take a seat. The sofa was a two-seater, the only size that would fit into the space, and so they were sitting close together but Fiona didn't mind.

She might have just met Tom the day before but she felt comfortable around him and he certainly seemed a decent guy.

'Thank you so much for your help,' Fiona said. 'How do you get Archie to listen to you?' she added.

Tom chuckled.

'Years of practice with truculent dogs.'

Fiona smiled. It was clear that Tom loved his job and his canine charges.

'Don't go thinking that Mr Dixon here was all sweet obedience when he first arrived,' he added.

Fiona chuckled. She couldn't imagine Dixon being anything other than highly trained.

'You don't believe me?' Tom asked, raising an eyebrow. Fiona shrugged. Surely he could see that it was hard to imagine Dixon as anything else.

'I was at the park with him, not long after I had him and he saw a squirrel. Seriously, you would think it was the first time he had ever seen one. And off he went, disappeared.'

'Where did you find him?'

'I didn't.'

Fiona frowned, gesturing to Dixon who was snoozing.

'I didn't find him. The dog warden did.' Fiona winced.

'Doesn't look so great if you're a dog trainer who has managed to lose his dog.'

Fiona giggled. It was a relief to know that she wasn't the only one to experience dog related disasters.

When Tom looked at her, she thought she had made a mistake, but then he laughed, too.

'Yeah, I think that story has done the rounds at work,' Tom said when their laughter had subsided. 'Not our finest hour, eh, Dixon?'

Dixon's ears pricked up and he walked over and rested his head in Tom's lap. Tom fussed his ears and Dixon made happy noises.

'So how did you get from chasing squirrels to this?' Fiona asked, a part of her hoping there was a well-kept secret that could transform the way Archie behaved by just muttering the right words.

'Lots and lots of work.'

Fiona nodded. She knew that would be the answer. And it wasn't as if she needed Archie to be as well trained as Dixon. She just needed to have some control over him.

'But don't worry. I'm guessing you just need some basics to get you through till your friend gets back.'

'Basics is fine. I don't want much, just maybe for him to listen to me once in a while and not to raid other people's picnics.'

Tom laughed again.and it was a good sound. Somehow it made Fiona feel better and that was something she needed right now.

'I'm sure we can do something about that. The trick is probably to prevent him getting off the lead, then you should be able to avoid any more picnic related or water related disasters.'

Fiona nodded. There was a question she wanted to ask but she didn't think she was brave enough.

Why was he helping her? She was a stranger to him and yet he was going out of his way to help her. Then a thought struck her and she had to clench her hands in her lap to prevent slapping herself across the forehead for being so foolish.

He was a professional and he would need to be paid. She couldn't believe she hadn't even thought about that and he had clearly been too polite to point out the fact.

'I'll pay you, of course,' Fiona said hurriedly.

Again Tom waved away the comment.

'Don't be daft. I offered to help you out. You don't offer to help and then bill someone for your time.'

'Please, this is your job and I'm taking up your time.'

'Look, if you really want to do something why not invite me round for a beer sometime in your garden?' Tom cleared his throat and he seemed uncomfortable, as if maybe he had crossed a line.

'That's a great idea. How about next Saturday?' The last thing Fiona wanted was for him to feel that way and besides, she wouldn't mind spending some time with him. He was a nice guy, who was helping her out and it was the least she could do.

'Great. Well, we'd best be heading off. Dixon needs a walk. Same time tomorrow?' Tom asked, getting to his feet.

'Sounds good,' Fiona said.

'I think we'll try Archie with a longer lead. I have a spare one to save you buying one.'

Fiona smiled.

'Perfect, thank you. We'll see you tomorrow.'

Fiona saw Tom out of the front door and then stood and watched him and Dixon walk away. She liked Tom but was she ready? Not that he had shown signs of wanting anything but friend-ship, of course. But he seemed keen to spend time with her and she knew that whatever her doubts, she wanted to spend time with him. But had she moved on enough to try? That was the question.

Waiting in Vain

Fiona couldn't quite believe it. She and Archie had managed to walk to the spot in the park where she had arranged to meet Tom, with no incidents. Archie had taken a fancy to a very pretty little Cavalier King Charles spaniel but the owner had stopped for both dogs to greet each other and then Archie had been happy to keep walking. What was almost more surprising was the fact that there was no sign of Tom or Dixon.

Fiona glanced at her watch. She was five minutes early but still ... The impression she had of Tom was that he was never late for anything; his life was too organised for that.

After fifteen minutes and repeatedly checking her phone for texts, Fiona sensed Archie was starting to get impatient and so she sent a quick text to say that she was going to walk Archie around the pond as he was showing signs of getting bored.

Boredom meant only one thing — Archie would start to look for something to do and that could only end in mischief.

Walking round the lake, Fiona knew deep down that Tom wasn't coming. She probably shouldn't be surprised. She was sure he had better things to do in his down time that give free dog training lessons to her.

Still, it rankled a bit that he hadn't even bothered to let her know. When they had completed their circuit and arrived back to the meeting point there was still no sign.

Archie looked up at her and he looked disappointed, or maybe, Fiona thought, she was just projecting her own feelings.

'Let's go home, shall we? I don't think they're coming.'

Archie did a sort of half whimper, half moan and Fiona bent down to fuss his ears.

'You've been such a good boy today, Archie, I'm sure I can rustle up some dog treats for you when we get in.'

Archie's ears pricked up and then Fiona was having to jog to keep up with him as he headed for home.

Archie was settled on his favourite spot on the sofa and Fiona had just plonked down beside him when her phone rang. She pulled it from her pocket and looked at the screen, expecting it to be Tom apologising for not being where he said he was going to be.

One look at the screen and it was Becky wanting to video chat. Becky's face swam into view, fuzzy at first but then clearer.

'Archie!' Becky shouted as Archie nudged Fiona's arm out the way so he could see the screen. He whined and proceeded to try to lick the screen.

'Archie baby! Mummy misses you!'

Fiona smiled and waited, knowing there was no point trying to have a conversation with Becky until she and

Archie had had their moment.

'I miss you, baby. And I'm going to get home as soon as I can. Now you sit back down and let me talk to Auntie Fi.'

Miraculously Archie did just that. He half curled up in Fiona's lap, half on the sofa, near enough so he could see his mum but not so close that Fiona couldn't talk to Becky.

'How's it going?' Fiona said, smiling at her friend, wishing that she could do more than dog sit to help out.

'Dad's still in High Dependency but seemed a little brighter today.'

'That's great news.'

'I'm not sure when I am going to be able to leave him.'

'Don't even think about it. You need to focus on your dad and if you're worried about Archie, he's fine. I'm taking good care of him.'

'I know you are,' Becky said hurriedly, 'I didn't mean that you weren't. It's just you've had him for nearly a week and I don't know when . . . '

Becky's voice broke and she stopped talking. Fiona could see she was going to cry.

'Becks, I only wish I could do more for you. I wish I could be there.'

'You've done plenty,' Becky said, managing a watery smile. 'You taking care of Archie means I have one less thing to worry about.'

Fiona felt a stab of guilt. She had been doing her best but had so far managed to 'lose' Archie at least four times. Admittedly she had found him but she wasn't sure that was the point.

'Oh no, Archie! Have you been up to mischief?'

Archie's ears went flat to his head and for the first time during the conversation, he turned his head away so he couldn't see Becky.

'Archie?' Becky said.

Archie whined and then tried to lick the screen.

'I'm so sorry, Fiona. I hoped he would be on his best behaviour.'

'It's fine, Becks, I don't want you to

37

worry about it.' Fiona's thoughts turned to Tom and his offer of help and then the fact that he had subsequently not turned up.

'What?' Becky said in a voice that told Fiona she had read whatever message her face was giving out without knowing.

'Just a guy I met in the park. He's a dog trainer and he's offered to give me and Archie a few lessons.'

'Really?' Becky said and she was now grinning. 'Throwing caution to the wind for a change. I approve.'

'He seems like a nice guy and you always said that you can tell a lot about a person by how they treat animals.'

'I did,' Becky said in a slightly smug voice.

'There's no need to make a big thing out of it. We're just meeting in the park to practise some dog training basics.'

'Uh huh,' Becky said with a wicked grin as Fiona felt her face flush at the thought that Tom was also going to come over for a drink.

'Enough about me. Tell me how your dad is,' Fiona said, changing the subject. She wasn't sure what to think about Tom. She wasn't sure what to make of him not turning up. Should she give him the benefit of the doubt?

★   ★   ★

Fiona stared at her phone, her finger hovering as she tried to decide whether she should click 'send' or not. She had written what she hoped was a no pressure text, just checking that Tom was OK and asking if they were still on for the next day.

Archie was fast asleep beside her and making little snuffling noises, as if he were having a particularly good dream.

'Should I send it, Archie?' she asked the dog softly. Archie's ear pricked up at the sound of his name and he opened one eye, scanned Fiona for signs of treats and then, grumbling, turned over and went back to sleep.

'You're no help,' Fiona said but she

couldn't help smiling. Although she had been worried about Archie from the moment he arrived, and in particular any time they stepped outside, she had to admit that it was nice to have some company in the evenings.

A picture appeared in her mind as she imagined herself with a dog of her own, highly trained just like Dixon and with perfect manners.

Unbidden, an image of Tom joined the fantasy and before she knew it, they were walking hand in hand with their dogs trotting along at their heels.

Fiona put her phone on charge and stepped back on to the sofa. She had no idea where that idea had come from. She barely knew Tom and he had already stood her up once. Was she really going to let herself be treated like that again — treated as if she wasn't important?

She shook her head at herself. Her mind was simply getting carried away with the fantasy of what life could be. She knew only too well that reality was often very different.

Archie moved and snuggled in next to her, with his head on her lap and she smoothed down his ruffled fur. No, she wasn't going to send the text. She wasn't going to make the first move. If Tom was a decent guy then he would contact her and explain. If he wasn't, then there was no way she was going to go chasing after him.

To the Rescue – Again!

Fiona normally enjoyed working from home. She got much more done than she ever had when she worked in an office. Being able to choose her own distractions, in her case a local radio station that played a mixture of music including some classical, and make a cup of tea when she wanted to, was bliss after the regimented call centre job.

Not only that but she was doing what she loved, designing and creating websites for people. However, today she was distracting herself. She had found herself checking her phone every ten minutes and as yet there was nothing from Tom.

'Maybe there never will be,' she said, directing her thoughts to Archie who was chewing on a plastic bone. He tilted his head on to one side as if he wasn't sure what she was going on about.

'Tom,' Fiona said. 'Maybe that's it and he's just going to disappear.'

Archie moved to her side and she reached down to give him a stroke.

'But we don't need him, do we, Archie? You and I can figure out how you can walk on a lead, can't we?'

Archie tossed his plastic bone into the air and it knocked the glass of water off Fiona's small fold down desk. Fortunately the glass didn't break, but Fiona couldn't help thinking it was an omen and that perhaps they did need Tom's help after all. Assuming he was willing to give it, of course.

At gone five o'clock there was still no message from Tom and Archie was definitely in need of a walk, judging by the number of times he had run in circles around Fiona's small flat. Fiona clipped on his lead and headed for the door.

'It's not like we're expecting to see them,' Fiona told Archie, who was more interested in getting the front door open. 'This is the time we normally go for a walk, so we might accidentally bump into them.'

Archie looked up from his scrabbling at the front door for a moment and Fiona knew she was kidding no-one with her excuses.

Mind you, it was clear that Archie was ready for a walk and so she should take him, whether there was a chance that they would meet Tom or not.

'Archie, please be good. I'm not sure I can cope with any of your shenanigans today.'

Archie gave what passed as a doggy smile and Fiona didn't feel reassured at all. With a sigh, she unlocked the front door and Archie burst forth, dragging her along behind him so that Fiona had to break into a sort of undignified trot.

By the time they reached the entrance to the park, Fiona was out of breath and very pink, with beads of sweat collecting at her hairline. She had spent all day hoping that she would casually bump into Tom at the park and now she was desperately hoping to get through Archie's walk without meeting a soul, particularly Tom.

Fiona and Archie completed their loop of the lake and miraculously Archie was still attached to his lead. If it hadn't been for the pace that Archie had been setting, Fiona would have said it had been an enjoyable walk.

It was certainly a relief to finally have a walk that did not involve her having to apologise to strangers and trying to remember her school French lessons.

Archie slowed his gallop, seeming intent on sniffing some grass and Fiona took the opportunity to catch her breath. It was good exercise she supposed but all she could think about was the hot shower and mug of hot chocolate that would be waiting for her once she got in.

With all thoughts focused on how good it would be to get into her fleecy pyjamas, Fiona didn't notice that Archie's lead had gone slack until she heard him barking. Not right next to her, where he should have been, but from some distance.

With a frustrated growl, she kicked her tired legs into gear and started to run off in the direction of the truculent pooch. A young couple seeing her running with a lead in her hand and no dog, smiled and gestured for her to run over one of the bridges that crossed the lake. She waved a thanks, not having enough breath to use actual words and crossed her fingers in the hope that Archie would not get into any mischief.

Across the bridge Fiona stopped, hands on her knees, catching her breath whilst she scanned that side of the park trying to spot Archie.

There were lots of people and plenty of dogs but no Archie. Fiona felt her annoyance fade and her anxiety increase. There was no sign of devastation and so no indication which direction Archie might have headed off in.

She stopped an older gentleman

walking an equally elderly dog, asking if he had seen Archie but the gentleman shook his head and wished her luck in finding Archie. This continued for what Fiona calculated was nearly an hour. She had gone from anxious to full blown panic, imagining all the things that could have happened to Archie.

Tears sprang to her eyes as the tiredness and the cold started to overwhelm her. She should have been paying more attention. It was all her fault and now she was going to have to tell Becky that she had managed to lose her beloved Archie.

Fiona thought she should call someone but she didn't know who. She knew the council had a dog warden but doubted that they worked into the evening. Maybe she should call the local animal shelter? They might have taken Archie in, if someone thought he was a stray.

Shakily, she drew her mobile from her pocket and tried to get an internet connection so that she could find the phone number. Her fingers were numb with cold, the sun was starting to set and she barely had a phone signal.

'Come on!' she hissed at her phone, as if that would help. A tear started to run down her cheek. She held her phone up in the air, in the vain hope of picking up a better signal.

'Excuse me?' a voice said behind her, but Fiona didn't have time to make small talk with some stranger.

'I think I have something you've lost.'

Fiona spun on her heel as Archie jumped up, making muddy paw-prints all over her jeans, but for once Fiona didn't care.

'Archie! Where have you been? I've been so worried!' Fiona knelt down and Archie gave her a hug, whilst licking her nose, which Fiona liked to think was his way of saying sorry.

'Thank you so much!' Fiona said, finally looking up at Archie's rescuer. She nearly overbalanced and would have landed bottom first in a puddle if Tom hadn't reached out a hand to steady her. He carefully helped Fiona to her feet.

Tom gave a sort of half smile.

'I was looking for you and Archie. I wanted to apologise about not making it yesterday and not letting you know. Dixon and I were just about to give up and then I saw a dog who looked suspiciously like Archie heading towards the exit.'

Fiona's eyes widened. If Archie had got out of the park — well, it didn't bear thinking about, since the park was surrounded by busy roads.

'How did you get him to stop?' Fiona asked.

'I let Dixon off the lead and he sort of rounded him up.'

Fiona raised an eyebrow, briefly wondering whether another dog would help with the Archie problem. She quickly dismissed it. If she couldn't handle Archie there was no guarantee that she would have any more luck with another dog. Archie would probably teach him bad habits!

'Are you OK?' Tom asked, looking concerned as Fiona realised that she had been silently thinking.

'Yes sorry, just relieved and . . . ' Fiona wanted to ask more about why Tom had stood her up but since he had just rescued her once more from an Archie disaster, it seemed a little churlish.

'Look, it's getting dark and cold, and I don't know about you but I'm starving. I know a dog-friendly pub that's not too far away. The food's always good and service is quick. Will you join me? I feel awful about yesterday.'

Fiona waved that away.

'You've rescued me and Archie too many times to worry about that.'

'I still feel bad, so please let me explain over a hot dinner.'

Fiona had to admit that sounded even better than her pyjamas and mug of hot chocolate that was waiting for her at home.

'Sounds good, but only if we can go

Dutch,' Fiona said. Tom raised an eyebrow.

'We can sort that out later,' he said with a mischievous grin that told Fiona there was no way she was going to be allowed to pay for her own dinner.

Tom started heading off with Archie on Dixon's lead and Dixon trotting beside him and so Fiona shrugged and caught up. It would be nice to have some company and she was curious as to why Tom hadn't even let her know that he wasn't coming.

Tom's description of the pub hadn't done it justice. It was on the corner of two main roads and from the outside, looked like every pub in London.

Inside, Fiona felt like she had been transported to the rolling hills of the countryside. There was a huge inglenook fireplace, with a fire blazing and horse brasses hanging from its heavy wooden lintel.

The floor was darker wood, worn with centuries of foot fall and no doubt stained with ale and beer. The tables and chairs looked antique but well cared for and most of the clientele had dogs with them and were wearing wellies. Fiona felt right at home.

Tom found them a table near to the fire so that they could warm up. Dixon lay down at his feet but Tom looped Archie's lead around a dog hook that had been attached to the underside of the table.

'I think you've had enough adventures for one day, young man,' Tom said, patting Archie on the head. Archie seemed to have worn himself out and so curled up in a tight ball next to Dixon.

Tom bought them drinks and ordered the food, before rejoining Fiona at the table.

'So about yesterday . . . '

'Really, it's fine,' Fiona said and she felt that now. She felt sure that Tom had a good reason and it wasn't as if they were dating or anything. He had just offered to help her out and if something else had come up that was fair enough.

Now she thought about it, there were probably loads of good reasons why he hadn't been able to contact her — lack of mobile phone signal for one. She smiled at him but Tom still looked troubled.

'Honestly, Archie and I needed to go for a walk so we waited for a bit and then went home.'

'I should have contacted you but I couldn't,' Tom said, which Fiona thought was probably an unnecessarily mysterious statement to make. She smiled and nodded though.

'I had to work and then I couldn't use my phone.'

Fiona nodded again, thinking that Tom was digging himself a bit of a hole. He was a dog trainer, after all, and she couldn't see that that created much in the way of emergencies, unless the dog you were dealing with was Archie, of course.

'It's fine, Tom. You don't need to explain,' Fiona said. She was curious, to be sure, but at the same time it was clear that Tom was undergoing some kind of internal battle, which she didn't want to add to.

Their food arrived and Tom had been right; it was delicious. Fiona had a homemade steak and ale pie, at Tom's suggestion, and it came with a pile of chips and fresh veg.

'So do you want to tell me what happened to Archie today?' Tom said and Fiona was a little relieved that he had decided to lay to rest his confusing explanation and that they could move on to safer ground.

'Just the usual. He was actually being really good other than wanting to walk faster than I did.'

Tom raised an eyebrow and Fiona thought he was adding that information to the list of things he needed to 'fix' in Archie's behaviour.

'He stopped to have a good sniff and I looked away for a second and the next thing, he was gone. He ran so fast and I couldn't see him . . . ' Fiona could feel some of the panic return at the memory.

'The first thing we will do is make sure that he comes to you when you call him. That way, if he does manage to escape his lead, he'll come straight back to you.'

Now it was Fiona's turn to raise an eyebrow. Tom must have magical powers if he thought he could make Archie do that.

'Look, I fixed Dixon's squirrel fascination and Archie is a smart boy, he just needs some direction.'

Fiona laughed.

'I think you have tremendous faith in Archie, not to mention me.'

'From what I've seen you can look after yourself very well,' Tom said, flashing Fiona a genuine smile.

A Walk in the Park . . .

It was hard to imagine a day that had turned so bad becoming one of Fiona's favourites for a long while. Tom had been great company, managing to be both funny and happy to talk about himself, as well as interested in Fiona and her life.

It was hard not to let her imagination run away with her. She couldn't remember the last time she had met someone that she felt so in tune with. And although she would never let on to Becky, she was feeling a little lonely since her best friend had had to head back home.

Even with Archie for company, it was nice to be able to talk to someone who could talk back.

Tom had suggested they meet at the park for Archie's first lesson the next morning. He said that it fitted better with his work schedule and since Fiona could make her own work schedule, she readily agreed.

Standing in front of the clothes rail that served as her wardrobe she knew she was being ridiculous. In truth she did have plenty of outfits that would do for dog walking.

She wasn't exactly focused on her appearance in general, especially since she had started working from home. But today it seemed like it was important.

Archie stood on the arm of the small sofa with his head cocked on one side as if he was trying to work out what Fiona was doing.

'I know I'm being ridiculous, Archie, but I'd still like to look my best.'

At that Archie leapt off the sofa and ran to a small plastic bag that was folded up in the corner. It contained various dog toys and Fiona assumed he wanted to play but instead Archie trotted back with his warm winter coat which he usually refused to wear.

'You want to dress up too?' Fiona said, reaching down and taking the coat from Archie. 'Are you trying to impress your new friend as well?'

Fiona held the coat up. It was blue and green tartan and she thought Archie looked very smart it in, when he wasn't trying to wriggle out of it.

'But I think Dixon would be more impressed if you didn't escape your lead and run off. I know I would be,' Fiona said, reaching down to stroke Archie's head. Archie twisted out of her way and tried to pull the dog coat from her arms.

'OK, OK, you can wear your coat but you have to help me choose my outfit.'

Having finally settled on a newish pair of jeans, a jumper and her navy gilet, Fiona and Archie headed off to the park. Fiona knew they were early but decided that it might be good if Archie ran off some of his energy before the lessons began, or that was the excuse she would give if she was asked.

To be honest, she hadn't been able to

settle to anything, all her thoughts on seeing Tom again, which she knew was ridiculous and that she was getting way ahead of herself but none of that seemed to matter to her heart.

With Archie trotting beside her in his posh coat, behaving for once, Fiona felt like she could do anything. Before they reached the lake, Fiona could see Tom in the distance. He was dressed casually as always but looked so handsome, even from a distance that Fiona felt her cheeks colour.

She could only hope that the pinkness would be mistaken for the glow of exercise and the autumn wind rather than embarrassment.

Dixon looked in their direction and then Tom spotted Fiona and Archie and raised an arm. Fiona waved back, feeling a little shy all of a sudden. Shaking her head at herself, she and Archie made their way over. Archie and Dixon sniffed each other and chased around in circles whereas Tom and Fiona settled for a simple hug.

'It's good to see you both,' Tom said, sounding as if he meant it. 'Are you ready to get started? I thought we could put Archie through his paces and then maybe get a coffee? I don't have to be at work until one.'

'Sounds good,' Fiona said, smiling back, thinking that it actually sounded perfect but then remembered she had to get through Archie's training without incident which seemed like a near impossible task, even with Tom at her side.

'Right, mister,' Tom said, addressing Archie, 'I'm going to put you on this long lead so you can't disappear. Tom handed the long lead to Fiona.

'We are going to practise simple recall,' Tom said although Fiona thought there was nothing simple about it where Archie was concerned. 'I'm going to show you and Archie how it's done with Dixon and then I want you to copy me.'

Fiona nodded and looked at Archie, silently begging him to behave.

Tom whistled at Dixon, who immediately appeared at his side.

'Right, I'm going to send Dixon away and then call him back. Dixon knows whistles and hand signals but we'll stick with words because I think it will be better for Archie.'

Tom raised an arm and Dixon gambolled off. Tom let him run and Fiona was a little worried that he had gone too far and they would never see him again.

'Dixon! Come!' Tom shouted firmly.

A blur of black appeared in the distance and then Dixon was there sitting in front of Tom, looking up adoringly.

'Good boy, Dixon,' Tom said and held out his hand which clearly contained some kind of tasty treat.

'Right, now it's your turn,' Tom said, turning to Fiona who could only look horrified.

'Do you think this is a good idea?' she asked, feeling the familiar panic start to bubble inside her. 'Archie

61

doesn't come back over small distances let alone if I send him away.'

'That's what the long lead is for,' Tom said reassuringly. 'Now,' he said, reaching into a small pouch that hung off his belt, 'show him his treat and then send him away.'

Fiona took the treat and realised that she had Archie's full attention, since he was trying to climb up her to get to it.

'Sit,' Tom said quietly but in a tone that brooked no argument and to Fiona's complete surprise, Archie did as he was told.

'Now send him away.'

Fiona made shooing signals but Archie was too focused on the treat.

'OK, try saying 'Away'.'

'Away!' Fiona said and Archie moved back a little. 'Go on! Away!'

Archie trotted away but kept looking over his shoulder, whereas Fiona kept looking at Tom, waiting for him to say it was OK to call Archie back. Archie had reached the tree line, and nearly the end of his lead.

'Call him back and make sure that you sound excited,' Tom instructed.

Fiona raised an eyebrow but did as she was told.

'Archie! Come here, boy!'

Archie continued his deep exploration of the nearest tree but Fiona was sure that his ears were cocked in her direction.

'And again. This time hold the treat up in the air.'

Fiona followed the instructions and to her surprise Archie turned to look at her. Seeing that she had his attention, she slapped both hands on her legs.

'Come on, Archie! See what I've got for you.'

Archie took a few steps in her direction and then started to run. Fiona stared in disbelief as Archie ran full pelt towards her.

'When he arrives, make him sit. He only gets the treat when he sits,' Tom said.

Archie leapt at Fiona as soon as he was near enough and Fiona would have fallen over, had Tom not grabbed her arm.

'Sit, Archie,' Fiona said once she had regained her balance and flashed Tom a grateful smile.

'No, you have to sit first,' she told Archie as he continued to jump up. Dixon got to his feet and moved in front of Tom before sitting down, as if to show Archie what he should be doing.

'Sit, Archie,' Fiona said one last time and he did. Fiona looked at Tom who smiled and gestured that she should give Archie his treat, which she did.

'Right, now make a real fuss of him. The key is making you more interesting than anything else he might come across on his travels.'

Fiona knelt down and Archie jumped into her arms. She scratched him behind the ears, in his favourite spot.

'That was brilliant, Archie, you are a star!' Fiona said. 'I can't believe it!' Fiona said, turning to Tom. 'Thank you.'

'It's a good start but we have to get him to a point when he will come back off the lead.' Tom smiled and Fiona thought that he was probably impressed that Archie had pulled if off for the first time.

For the next hour they repeated the exercise and Archie seemed content to go away and come back but Fiona was dreading the suggestion of taking him off the long lead.

'Well, I think Archie has got the hang of it but I suggest we stop now and have a coffee.'

Fiona let out her held in breath and Tom laughed.

'We won't let him off until you are confident,' Tom said.

Fiona thought that Tom would be teaching Archie for the rest of his life since she doubted she would ever feel that confident, but now she thought about it, that didn't seem like such a bad thing.

'That might take a while,' Fiona replied.

Tom shrugged.

'Fine by me.' And Fiona felt a fizz of something build up in her chest and she had to fight to keep her face from revealing her feelings.

'Coffee and cake is on me today,' Fiona said by way of a distraction, 'and no arguments.'

Tom raised a hand in the direction of the coffee shop and they headed towards it.

'Let's put Archie on a short lead, shall we?' Tom said, glancing at his watch.

Fiona nodded gratefully. She didn't want to be the one to say it but they weren't getting very far, very fast.

Once on the short lead, Archie seemed to get the message. When they reached the coffee shop, Fiona ordered the drinks and two blueberry muffins before joining Tom and the dogs at one of the outside tables.

'So you have a training job this afternoon?' Fiona asked as she settled herself into her seat.

'Uh-huh,' Tom said a little distractedly. 'How's the film maker's website going?'

Fiona was flattered that he had remembered such detail about her but also a little flummoxed by the fact that he didn't appear to want to talk about his job. He seemed happy to talk about all sorts of aspects of his life but not work. All he was succeeding in doing was to pique her interest.

She wondered if he just thought she might be bored by it, but that seemed strange since she and Archie were benefiting from his expertise. Perhaps a quick internet search once she was back home was in order. If Tom didn't want to talk about his work, a quick look for a website would surely allay her curiosity.

Why All the Secrecy?

Fiona knew she should be working. It wasn't as if she didn't have plenty to do. For once, Archie was snoozing on the sofa. Clearly all that exercise had worn him out. But despite all that, Fiona could not concentrate on anything. She had googled dog training in London but could find no trace of Tom. Then she had Googled his name and still nothing.

Fiona knew how hard it was to not be on the internet somewhere these days. Even if you didn't use it yourself, you could still turn up on other people's social media but there was no trace of Tom at all.

The more Fiona tried to believe that there was a logical explanation, the worse she felt. Was Tom lying about who he was and what he did? For the life of her she couldn't think of a single reason why he would do that.

They weren't due to meet until the following evening and so at least Fiona had some time to think over what she would do next.

Fiona was up early the next day and took Archie for a quick constitutional around the park. She had a meeting to attend in the city and she wanted to make sure that he would be OK for the few hours she would be away. Dressed in her only suit and feeling like she was playing a character, she took one last look in the mirror.

'What do you think, Archie? Do I look like a successful web designer?'

Archie leapt off the sofa and before Fiona could even squeal he had jumped up and left a trail of slightly damp paw-prints all down the front of her grey suit trousers.

She couldn't bring herself to tell him off — she should have known better than to call his name. Archie looked a little crestfallen so she reached down and scratched him behind the ears.

'Not your fault, buddy,' she said, flashing him a smile before she headed for the bathroom and hoped that the paw-prints would dry without leaving a mark.

'Right, I'm off,' she told Archie as she looked at her watch. Realising what the time was she let out a shriek, grabbed her bag and ran for the front door.

On the whole, Fiona was not a fan of the underground. She much preferred to travel by bus but since she was late today, she knew that the Tube was the best option. With any luck, and without any incidents, she would still reach her meeting with new clients on time.

Fiona rode the escalator up to the station at Regent Street, keeping to the left, since she had no desire to try to run in her low heels.

In her head she rehearsed her sales pitch. She knew she had some good ideas for the website and the clients had seemed keen on her suggestions but she knew better than to take anything for granted.

As she neared the top of the escalator she could see that people were all bunched up into a crowd and with a sigh she assumed that some of the automatic gates were not working.

One glance at her watch told she still had 15 minutes before her meeting was due to start and she knew it was only a few minutes' walk but still she couldn't help but tap her foot impatiently as she joined the slow moving queue.

Fiona couldn't really see what was happening as she seemed to be standing behind a group of exceptionally tall people. At last it was her turn to flash her oyster card at the automatic gate, which sprung open and let her through. It was only then that she spotted the reason for the delay. A group of police officers were stopping people to speak to them.

This was not unusual but Fiona had to bite back a sigh. She knew they were only doing their jobs but still, why did it have to be today? Why did it have to be this station?

Off to the side a couple were in discussion with a police officer as Fiona moved forward. It was then she spotted a springer spaniel, pulling on his lead and sniffing at people as they went past.

Fiona had to resist the urge to reach out and pet the dog. He seemed so friendly but she knew he was working and should be left to it. The dog quickly turned his attention to the man walking behind her and so Fiona walked forward to get out of the way.

Another police officer appeared and he was accompanied by a black spaniel. As Fiona reached the exit, the black spaniel surged forward and barked once. Fiona stared down at it.

'Would you mind stepping over here miss?' a voice said.

All Fiona could do was stare at the spaniel. What on earth could it have reacted to? Fiona knew that police dogs were trained to sniff out all sorts of things but she also knew that she had no offending articles on her. Not even any bank notes, since she rarely carried more than a little loose change.

'As you can see, miss, the dog has indicated . . . ' The voice trailed off and for the first time Fiona looked up and saw someone that she recognised. The face was so out of place and unexpected that she was convinced she was merely seeing things.

She had spent all morning thinking about Tom and now she was imagining him here as a police officer! She really was losing the plot. She blinked and looked up again, from the officer to his dog and back to the officer and then she knew she wasn't dreaming.

Fiona stared. The black spaniel was now sitting by the officer's leg in a position that was all too familiar. Fiona looked up once more to the officer's face and knew there was no mistake. Uniforms might make everyone look alike but she would know that face anywhere, she had been dreaming about it since she met him.

Fiona opened her mouth to speak

but no words came. In truth she had no idea what to say. To discover the truth about Tom's real job was one thing, but for Dixon to indicate that she had something on her that she shouldn't was beyond mortifying, even though she knew it couldn't be true.

Tom seemed to be having similar issues. He looked as if he wanted to say something but, like Fiona, had no idea what words to use. The silence seemed to stretch out between them.

'Sarge?' A young female officer appeared beside Tom. 'Did Dixon indicate on this lady?'

Fiona could feel her cheeks colour. This could not be happening. It had to be some kind of mistake. In any other circumstances she would be a little flustered and embarrassed but this was unreal. This was in front of Tom.

Fiona risked a look in his direction but he was still staring at her and Fiona wondered if he couldn't believe what was happening either. Maybe he thought she was carrying something

74

illegal. That thought was worse than anything else.

'Sarge?' the other officer said, looking curiously from Tom to Fiona and back again. 'Are you OK?'

That seemed to finally wake Tom up from his stupor.

'I'm fine, Georgie, thanks. This is a client of mine from dog training. Dixon was just happy to see her and forgot he was at work for a moment.'

Georgie nodded slowly and then the other officer with a sniffer dog beckoned her over and she left them to it.

Fiona tried to swallow the lump in her throat. She was relieved that there was an explanation but hurt by the fact that Tom had introduced her as a client. She supposed she was, really, but still she had thought that they had become friends over the last week but it was clear that Tom didn't feel that way.

'I have a meeting to get to,' Fiona said, making a show of checking her watch. Her looked of alarm was genuine as she would now have to hurry to make it there on time.

'Of course, sorry,' Tom said. 'Sorry about Dixon and the misunderstanding.'

Fiona nodded, wondering if Tom was going to say anything else but what followed was more silence and the sensible part of her brain was telling her to hurry up so she walked briskly away without even a look back.

Fiona did her best to push her thoughts and feelings aside. Right now she needed to focus on work. She could try to make sense of what had just happened later.

* * *

Fiona caught the bus home. No longer in a hurry, she preferred to travel with a view. She tried to ignore the voice in her head that told her she was avoiding the Tube station in case she met Tom again.

The meeting had gone well and she was confident that she had won an important piece of business so now she could afford to think about Tom. He wasn't a dog trainer, or at least not in the sense that he had made her believe. He trained police dogs and he was a police officer.

Fiona looked out of the window from the top deck of the bus and watched the people scurrying around going about their business. What she really couldn't understand was why he hadn't just told her.

Maybe not on their first meeting but surely at the pub or the coffee shop would have been a good time? It made sense now that she hadn't been able to find Tom on the internet. If he trained police dogs he would have no reason to advertise and she guessed as an officer a low profile was probably a good thing.

Was that why he had played so coy? Fiona had never really met a police officer. She had once had her bike stolen and gone in to her local station back home to report it but that was it.

She admired people for wanting to

do the job but had never even considered doing the job herself, way too scary and unpredictable for her. But you had to be impressed that some people were prepared to face that, to help people.

Fiona reached her stop.

'Thank you,' she said to the driver as she went, somewhat distractedly.

Perhaps she could understand why Tom might be reluctant to talk about work but the fact that he had lied by omission did not sit well with her.

It reminded her too much of Mark and that was not someone she wanted to spend any time thinking about. She was supposed to be meeting Tom later for Archie's next lesson so maybe she would just wait and see what he had to say for himself.

Mixed Emotions

Archie seemed more bouncy than usual and so all Fiona's energy was focused on getting to the meeting place without him getting up to mischief or doing his Houdini routine. She kept the lead tight around her wrist and although Archie was pulling and wriggling, as if he was desperate to escape, she managed to get to the spot by the lake without incident.

'Sit, Archie,' Fiona said but all Archie seemed to want to do was dance. He was hopping from one paw to another in what Fiona thought looked a bit like a rain dance.

Thankfully, it wasn't working. The sky had the clear blueness that signalled the best kind of October late afternoon. The sun was low but it had been shining all day and it was the kind of warm mellowness that Fiona loved.

Archie started to bark and pull on his

lead and before Fiona could do anything he had done a tuck and roll that an Olympic gymnast would be proud of, and he was gone, racing away from her towards a figure with an accompanying black dog.

Well, at least he is running towards Tom, Fiona thought. Hopefully he could catch him. Fiona started to jog in their direction, almost glad that Archie had done his party trick as at least it was a bit of a distraction from what Fiona assumed would be an awkward meeting.

Fiona stopped when she realised that Tom had Archie, figuring that she would wait where she was, now that Archie's escape act had been curtailed.

Fiona's phone rang in her pocket and she was tempted to ignore it but a thought crossed her mind that it might be Becky and so she pulled it from her pocket and answered.

'Why don't you try and call him? We can see if he remembers his previous lesson.' Fiona pulled the phone away from her ear long enough to see that Tom's name had come up. She frowned, no hello — nothing. 'Fiona?'

'Yes, sorry. Will do,' she said, hoping she was managing a breezy tone. Fiona shook her head at herself. Just get on with it, she told herself firmly. Hanging up and putting her phone back into her pocket she took a deep breath. She focused all her thoughts on Archie and then held up her arm.

'Archie! Here, boy!' she called, clapping her hands on her knees. Archie was too busy dancing around Dixon to take any notice but at least Dixon was playing his part. He was sitting right next to Tom's leg, all his attention focused on Fiona and doing his best to ignore Archie, which was not easy since Archie had now decided to hang off one of Dixon's ears.

Fiona remembered the packet of treats she had in her pocket and pulled them free before rattling them in the air. This at least made Archie stop and turn to look at Fiona. Fiona rattled them one more time.

'Archie, come here!'

Fiona held her breath as Archie took a few slow steps in her direction. She could feel herself smiling as she called one more time. Archie picked up pace and Fiona crouched down spreading her arms wide as Archie launched himself at her.

Without Tom to balance her, Fiona fell backwards leaving Archie standing on her chest and licking her face. Fiona was laughing and scratching Archie's ears, when Tom's face swam into view.

'Are you OK?' Tom asked, sounding concerned which just made Fiona laugh more.

'Are you kidding, he actually came back to me and he wasn't even on the long lead. I'm fantastic!'

Tom smiled and held out a hand and hauled her to her feet. Tom's grip was somehow firm but gentle and Fiona found herself pulled close to him. It seemed neither of them wanted to let go of each other and so they stood together, staring at each other like they were frozen in time.

Even Archie didn't run off. It seemed he had figured out how this all worked and he was due a treat. But it also didn't mean he was going to wait for ever. An impatient bark seemed to bring both Tom and Fiona back to the real world. Tom cleared his throat and opened the packet of treats.

'Get him to sit first,' Tom said as Fiona was so flustered she would probably just have thrown Archie the whole packet and told him to get on with it.

'Right, sit, Archie,' Fiona said, glad to have a reason to look away as she was sure that she was blushing. Archie did more dancing and Fiona looked at him with one eyebrow raised, before he sat down and looked up expectantly.

'Good boy,' she said, holding out a treat in her hand which he wolfed down and Fiona reached for his lead.

'Well, that was excellent,' Tom said, although whether he meant Archie or what had just happened between them, Fiona wasn't sure.

'He came back,' Fiona said, still wondering if she had dreamed the whole thing, including the part with Tom.

'He did. I think he has got recall sorted. So let's move on to some other commands.'

Fiona nodded. She wasn't too caught up in the moment to realise that Tom had avoided the subject of his job and what happened earlier. There would be time for that after. She would suggest they have a coffee or maybe she would invite Tom back to her place for that beer.

Right now, Tom seemed keen to focus on Archie and Fiona couldn't blame him. She felt like they were making real progress and Tom was right to concentrate on that while they could.

Archie was turning out to be a good student, at least if there were treats involved. He would now sit on command and even lie down sometimes. He had been off the lead for well over half an hour and Fiona hadn't lost him once — pretty impressive considering she had managed to lose him more than once when he was on the lead.

'Well, I think that's probably enough for one day,' Tom said as Archie executed a perfect sit to lie down. 'If you get a chance it would be worth practising the sit and down at home.'

'We will. I can't believe how well he's doing.'

'He had it in him and you just need to know the right tools,' Tom said with a smile. There was silence for a moment as Fiona tried to work out whether it was a good idea to suggest a coffee or a beer.

'Do you fancy . . . ' Fiona started to say just as Tom spoke.

'Well, we'd better be going,' he said.

'Of course,' Fiona said, cursing herself for not being more patient and reading the signs. It was clear that Tom was keen to go and perhaps she needed to pay attention to that.

Maybe all he had ever wanted was to help her with Archie and here she was continually suggesting that they spend time together outside the lessons. She felt foolish and in that moment all she wanted to do was go home and hide.

'Sorry,' Tom said with a slight frown, 'did you say something?'

'It's nothing,' Fiona said, forcing a smile on to her face. It wasn't Tom's fault if she had got the wrong idea. 'You and Dixon have a good evening,' she added, tugging on Archie's lead whilst trying to take a step away.

Tom said nothing but Fiona could feel him staring at her.

'You, too, Fiona. I'll see you Friday morning for another lesson.'

'Sounds great,' Fiona said, trying to force some cheerfulness into her voice and hide the fact that she felt like crying.

'Great. See you then,' Tom said and Fiona wasn't so far away that she couldn't detect a note of something in his tone. Disappointment? She shook her head.

She was only going to make things worse if she kept thinking like that. Tom was clearly not interested in her, perhaps not even wanting to be friends. He was probably just thrown off by her abrupt departure which was not too far away from being rude.

* * *

Fiona tried to throw herself into her work. She had won the contract to design the website for the Regent Street business and that was a big deal. She should have been excited and ready to get to work but all she felt like doing was moping around her flat, even though she knew she was behaving like a heartbroken teenager.

'It's just because I'm missing Becky,' Fiona told Archie who was curled up beside her on the sofa. Archie whined when he heard Becky's name and Fiona felt guilty — guilty that she was making

Archie sad and guilty for letting her imagination run away with her.

What had really happened, after all? She had met Tom at the park and he had been kind enough to offer to help her with Archie for free. They had spent a bit of time together at the pub and then Tom seemed happy to go back to being trainer and trainee.

Fiona sighed and sipped her coffee. Tom had only changed when she had bumped into him whilst he was working at a job that he seemed to have deliberately kept from her. That didn't really make sense to her.

Maybe he had simply decided that he wanted to help Fiona but nothing more. If that was the case then she really did need to get a grip. That was his prerogative and it wasn't as if Tom had really given any signs otherwise.

'I really must get on with some work,' she told Archie firmly who promptly rolled on his back and looked as if he was going to work on his snoring.

She had 24 hours before she was due

to meet with Tom again and she needed to make sure that she could handle it. The last thing she wanted to do was embarrass herself — or him, for that matter. If Tom wanted to keep it professional, then that was exactly what Fiona was going to do.

The Best Laid Plans . . .

Fiona and Archie arrived at the park early and Fiona started to put Archie through his paces. Archie seemed content to sit and lie down as long as there was a tasty treat on offer. Fiona knew that she should practise letting Archie off the lead but didn't think she was brave enough just yet. If Archie ran off and didn't come back then her plan to keep it professional was over before it started. Getting rescued by Tom again would not be helpful.

Archie was sitting in front of Fiona staring at her right hand that contained the treat but one eye keep looking off to the right and Fiona was sure that he had spotted Tom and Dixon.

Determined to follow her plan, she didn't look up herself although she was desperate to. She wanted to look at Tom to see if she could tell what he was thinking but she resisted. Instead, she concentrated on Archie.

'Down, boy,' Fiona said firmly but by now Archie's attention was all on Tom and Dixon. Fiona waved the treat in front of Archie's nose and at least got to see him sniff it momentarily before he looked back to his friends. Archie's tail wagged and it was clear that he was itching to run and greet them but somehow he was just about managing to contain himself.

'That's great work, Fiona, well done.'

Fiona's face glowed but this time it was more pride in how far she and Archie had come rather than embarrassment. Maybe it was going to be easier than she thought to play it professional.

Tom was by her side and Dixon was sniffing at her hand. She bent down to give him a proper stroke and to give herself a few more precious seconds to compose herself before she needed to talk to Tom. Archie was giving Tom his usual greeting which involved jumping up and down and barking.

'Well, I think we have the next area to work on,' Tom said as Fiona stood up. She took in the muddy paw prints on Tom's jeans and winced, although part of her thought it must be an occupational hazard of working with dogs.

Since Dixon was sitting patiently back by Tom's legs Fiona thought that most trained police dogs probably didn't behave like Archie.

She managed a smile and Tom seemed unbothered so she made a decision to stop worrying about such things. Tom had offered to help her and Archie and that was what he was doing.

They worked solidly for nearly an hour. Tom and Dixon would walk away, out of sight and Fiona would keep Archie close and give him the command for down.

Tom and Dixon would then come back to say hello and it was Fiona's job to keep Archie sitting down and calm.

It was not as easy as some of the other things that Archie had learned.

He seemed perfectly well behaved until Tom and Dixon got near and then he forgot his training and his manners and gave them both an effusive and muddy greeting.

'I think we are going to need to practise that one some more,' Tom said as Archie tried to greet him with a full body hug.

'I'm sorry,' Fiona said, feeling the all too familiar embarrassment return.

'Don't be. Most dogs have an Achilles heel when it comes to training. Dixon's is squirrels and it seems Archie just loves to greet people enthusiastically. It will just take some more practice.'

Since Tom didn't appear bothered by the prospect of spending more time with her and Archie, Fiona smiled.

'I really appreciate you doing all this,' she said, wondering if she should offer to pay for his time if they were going to be truly professional about this.

'My pleasure,' Tom said, smiling at her. Fiona was starting to feel confused again. He was once more giving the impression of enjoying being with her. Talk about mixed messages.

'We still on for those beers in your lovely garden tomorrow night?' Tom said. There was no sign of any concern in his voice.

As if the fact that they had an extremely awkward meeting when he was at work, doing a job that he had kept secret, had not happened. And that was all in addition to the fact that he had also given the impression that he wanted to keep it professional.

'Of course,' Fiona said, hoping that she wasn't giving away her surprise.

'Great,' Tom said and Fiona knew that was her cue to make some sort of plans.

'How about half five?'

'Let's make it six and I'll bring a takeaway. Do you prefer Indian or Chinese?'

Fiona wasn't sure what was happening but she knew she should be the one arranging the takeaway, not to mention paying for it.

'Whatever you like,' was all she could think to say.

If Tom was picking up on anything he said nothing, but merely smiled.

'Sounds great. Looking forward to it.'

'Me too,' Fiona said although to be honest she had no idea what she felt about it, since her emotions felt like they had been shoved in a washing machine and put on a top spin.

Tom whistled and Dixon trotted off beside him. Archie pulled at his lead, wanting to go with them.

'Come on, Archie, you'll be seeing them tomorrow, I guess.'

One pull on the lead and Archie fell into step beside her and Fiona could feel him gazing up at her.

'It's not just me, right?' she said to him. A young couple walking past gave her a funny look but she ignored them. Archie barked but Fiona had no idea if he was agreeing with her or telling her that she was losing the plot.

★　★　★

Fiona made herself work on Saturday morning to make up for the lost time she had spent mooning over Tom.

Once she had moved the new project on sufficiently she popped out to the shops and bought some beer and a pudding and then took Archie for his walk.

She was no clearer on what was happening between her and Tom.

It had started out promising, certainly a friendship and maybe more in time but then Tom had seemed to retreat to safer professional ground, then yesterday he had seemed all friendly again.

It was enough to make Fiona feel dizzy and despite the fact that she had spent a lot of time trying to work out what was going on, she had come to no conclusions.

Instead she had simply decided to go with the flow, not something that sat well with her. She liked to know where she stood, particularly after her previous experiences.

At six on the dot, Fiona took a deep breath just as the door buzzer sounded. She went to the door and Tom stood there, looking as handsome as ever, particularly since he was wearing a broad grin on his face.

'Evening,' he said.

'Hi! It's good to see you,' Fiona said, hoping she hadn't sounded too enthusiastic. She stood back to allow Dixon and Tom to enter and they all headed for her flat.

Fiona had shut Archie out in the garden to make sure he didn't try to escape with both doors open. He was now putting on a stellar performance the other side of the patio doors, leaping up at them and leaving behind smeared paw-prints, not to mention the high-pitched barking he was making.

Tom laughed.

'OK, so we definitely need to work on that.' He walked to the patio door and looked down at Archie, whose frenzied movements seemed to increase.

Tom held up a hand and said

nothing. Archie seemed to realise that he was going to get nowhere behaving as he was and sat down, although his bottom was still wriggling.

Tom held up a treat and then he pulled open the door. Archie trotted in and sat down, much to Fiona's amazement, and waited to be handed his treat.

'You are so good with him,' Fiona said softly, not wanting to break the spell that had fallen over them all.

'He's a smart cookie, which helps,' Tom said, looking up at from his spot on the floor where he and Archie were play fighting.

Dixon had inched over and Tom gave him the signal to say that he could join in. Fiona laughed and went to fetch a couple of beers from the fridge and took them out to the two metal chairs that were set on the small patio. Tom joined her.

'I've ordered Indian and they are going to deliver at about seven.'

'Perfect — I'll pay, though,' Fiona added.

'Too late, it's already paid for,' Tom said, raising an eyebrow as if to challenge Fiona to argue, even though it was clearly pointless.

'You shouldn't have, this was supposed to be my treat.'

'You've bought the beer and provided the ambiance.'

Now it was Fiona's turn to raise an eyebrow.

'Look, my mum always told me to never turn up as a guest empty handed. Admittedly I don't have the takeaway with me but it is coming.' He grinned at Fiona.

'And my mum taught me to not to take help for granted.'

'Who says you are taking me for granted?' Tom said and there was a wicked glint in his eye. It made Fiona smile.

'What I mean is that it's your job and since you aren't letting me pay you then you should at least let me buy dinner.'

'Well, if you insist you can buy dinner next time.'

Fiona took a swig of beer to hide her surprise.

'Assuming you are happy to do this again?' Tom's smile had fallen a little and now he looked like Fiona had felt the other day.

'I'd love to,' she said and they clinked bottles.

Fiona was just trying to work up to asking him about his job and the whole awkward meeting when Tom's phone beeped. The look on his face told Fiona it was probably not a welcome distraction.

'Sorry, do you mind?' he said, pulling his phone from his pocket.

'Go for it,' Fiona said as Archie trotted up with a tennis ball in his mouth. He dropped it at her feet and Fiona threw it down the length of the garden laughing as both Archie and Dixon went racing for it.

It was only then that she realised that Tom had stepped back into the flat.

Fiona had thrown the ball a couple of times before Tom reappeared.

100

'I'm really sorry but I'm going to have to cut and run.'

'Oh, OK,' Fiona said, not knowing what else to say. Tom looked disappointed so that was something.

'Of course,' Fiona said, getting to her feet. 'At least let me pay for the takeaway if you're not going to get to eat any of it.'

'No, please. I am being incredibly rude leaving like this but please believe I would much rather stay here with you.'

Fiona felt like his gaze was searching her face for her reaction.

'Tom, I understand, really I do. Sometimes things come up, work for instance.'

Now it was Fiona's turn to study his face but she could see no indication of what the 'something' was. Tom merely looked frustrated and his jaw was forming a hard line so Fiona decided now was not the time to ask.

'I'll text you tomorrow. Maybe we can meet up for some dog training,'

Tom said as he picked up his jacket. Dixon was at his side in an instant.

'That would be lovely but no pressure. Just let me know,' Fiona said as Tom nodded distractedly and then he was gone.

And Fiona was left to another Saturday night in, in front of the TV with only Archie for company and a lot to think about.

Another Woman

Somehow, Deep down, Fiona knew that she would not hear from Tom on Sunday. It made sense if he had been called into work, she supposed. No doubt it had been a late night and she doubted he would have felt like meeting her for more dog training.

There was a small thought that nagged at her though. Why hadn't he simply said he had to go to work? The fact that he hadn't, made her mind race as she considered other possibilities.

'Stop it!' she told herself firmly. 'Not every man is like Mark.'

Archie looked up and she knew it was time to take him for a walk.

'Come on then. We'll get some practice in so you can show off next time we see Tom.'

It was another perfect October day. The sun was shining and there were plenty of people and dogs out enjoying the good weather.

Archie seemed content to trot beside her as they made their usual lap of the park and Fiona didn't think life got much better than this.

They passed the coffee shop and then all of a sudden Archie was pulling on his lead.

Fiona shifted her grip to make sure that he didn't manage to escape and tried to work out exactly what he was after. She couldn't see any other dogs and there were no squirrels in sight. In fact nothing but a couple walking away from her down the path that led off to the right.

'What's going on, Archie?' Fiona said, reaching down with her free hand to pat Archie on the head. He looked up at her and then back to the couple walking away and started to pull again on his lead, this time barking.

The woman in the couple turned around as Archie whined. The man flashed them a quick look and then

Fiona knew exactly why Archie was barking. He wanted to go and see his friend and trainer. It was Tom.

Fiona didn't wait to see Tom's reaction. Instead she started walking in the other direction. Archie wasn't keen at first but seemed to get the message quickly that they would not be meeting up with Tom that day.

Fiona's mind raced but the main thing she felt was foolish and all she wanted to do was go home. Perhaps Tom hadn't realised it was them. She shook her head. That was a ridiculous thought as she was sure he would have recognised Archie.

When she got home she gave Archie a few more treats than normal. He had been well behaved and they had managed to do the whole walk without incident, as long as Fiona ignored the fact that Tom had been at the park with another woman.

Her phone beeped and Fiona wondered if it would be Tom offering some sort of explanation, or maybe he didn't think he had done anything wrong.

She didn't have any time to continue with the thought as the screen lit up to say it was Becky.

Fiona threw herself on to the sofa, patted the seat beside her so that Archie jumped up and answered. For the first few minutes there was just Archie whining and barking and Becky talking to him.

When Archie finally settled down to simply stare at the screen lovingly, it was Becky and Fiona's turn to talk.

'How's it going?' Fiona asked as she tried to push aside all that had happened that afternoon.

'About the same. They say Dad's stable and that it will take time. I wouldn't want to be anywhere else right now but it's getting tough. All I seem to do is work on my laptop and sit beside his bed.'

Fiona nodded. That was tough and much worse than anything she imagined she was going through — especially since she suspected that much of it was happening in her head.

She was behaving like she and Tom were dating, which of course they weren't, and he was free to do whatever he liked and Fiona didn't really have a cause to moan about it, or act all hurt for that matter.

'Earth to Fiona? Come in, Fiona?'

'Sorry,' Fiona said, 'do you want me to bring Archie up to you for a few days? We could keep you company and I know Archie would love it.'

'I'd love to see you!' Becky's eyes lit up at the thought. 'But it's a long way to come, Fi. Not to mention expensive.'

'Archie and I can come by train and besides since you've been away I have no social life so it's not like I've been spending any money.'

Fiona smiled. It was just what she needed. A few days away and a proper catch up with her best friend. Hopefully the time away and a frank discussion with Becky would set her back on the right track.

'We'll come tomorrow. I'll check the

train times and then let you know what time we are due to arrive.'

'Perfect!' Becky beamed, the first proper smile Fiona had seen for ages. 'What about work?' she added, the smile slipping a bit.

'Like you, I can work anywhere,' Fiona said. 'I'll work while you are with your dad and I'll have dinner on the table when you get home. I might even stretch to a bottle of wine.'

Becky clapped her hands together and Archie seemed to have picked up that something was happening. He stood up and started to wag his tail furiously.

'What do you think about a visit to your mum, Archie?'

Archie barked and started to do a little dance.

'Well, I think we are all in agreement. See you tomorrow, Becks,' Fiona said.

'Let me know what time you're going to arrive and I'll come and pick you up in Dad's car.'

'Brilliant. See you soon!'

Fiona hung up and switched on her laptop to check train times. This was what she needed and by the looks of it, Becky needed it too. She would go away for a few days, provide some moral support to her best friend and give herself some time to sort her own head out.

*   *   *

Archie had trotted by Fiona's side to the bus stop and made no fuss when he was asked to climb on the bus.

'You know, Archie, your mum is going to be so impressed with all the new things you have learned.'

Archie licked Fiona's nose which she took as a sign that he agreed.

'It's going to be nearly three hours on the train though, so you are going to have to be good.'

As if on cue, Archie settled down and looked like he was going to fall asleep.

At King's Cross, Fiona and Archie got on to their train and headed for

Sheffield. Fiona could feel a bubble of excitement at seeing her friend.

She had been gone for over two weeks and Fiona had really missed having her just down the road. As they both worked from home, they frequently met for lunch and it was a good way of breaking up the day.

She had also been worried about her friend up in Sheffield coping with her poorly dad on her own.

Becky's dad had moved to Sheffield after Becky had gone to university so she didn't know many people and Fiona knew that it had been tough for her.

Each time the train stopped, Archie would raise his head to look out of the window. When he realised that they weren't getting off there, he would sigh and settle back to his dozing.

He was being such a good boy that Fiona couldn't help feeling proud of him, not to mention thankful for all Tom's help.

Fiona picked up her phone and sent

Tom a text, explaining that she had decided to visit Becky with Archie and that she would let him know when she was back.

She didn't mention anything about seeing him in the park. If there was an explanation it was up to him to offer it and right now she needed to focus on Becky.

When the guard announced that the next stop was Sheffield, Fiona got to her feet and grabbed hold of the lead.

'Come on then, Archie,' she said. They walked down the aisle and waited for the train to stop.

Archie was jumping up trying to see out of the door window and Fiona couldn't blame him. She was excited, too.

They stepped on to the platform and Archie was off. The lead seemed to slip through Fiona's hand but she had spotted Becky and so let Archie run.

Archie jumped into Becky's arms whimpering and barking.

'Oh, I've missed you,' Becky said and

Fiona was close enough to see that Becky had tears in her eyes and she knew she had made the right decision to come.

'Missed you, too,' Fiona said with a smile, as Becky shifted Archie into one arm and they had a group hug.

'Let's get you back to Dad's,' Becky said, looking at her watch.

'Have you seen him today?'

'I popped in this morning but I'll head straight back once I drop you off, if you don't mind?'

'Of course not. Archie and I will be fine. You don't need to worry about it.'

'It's just that they say being there and talking to him could really help.'

Fiona reached out for her friend's hand and gave it a squeeze.

'You don't need to explain. Archie and I came to support you, not to make life more difficult. All you need to do is point us in the direction of some shops and let us know what time you're coming home and we'll be waiting for you.'

'Thanks. You have no idea how much I appreciate this. Tonight we can have a proper catch up and you can tell me exactly what is going on with you,' Becky said, unlocking the car door and stepping back to let Archie jump in.

Fiona climbed in to the passenger seat and once more marvelled at her best friend's ability to pick up on what she didn't say.

A Friend in Need

Fiona had cooked a lasagne and bought some salad, garlic bread and a nice bottle of red wine. She looked at her watch. It was late but Becky had said she would text as she left which would give Fiona enough time to warm up dinner and think about how she was going to explain the Tom situation without sounding like a crazy person.

'The thing is, Archie, when I say it out loud, I think I do sound crazy.'

'Not as crazy as talking to my dog,' Becky said, coming in through the front door, looking exhausted but happy to see them both. Archie ran up and Becky scooped him up into her arms.

'I remembered I was supposed to be texting when I drove out of the car park and at that point all I wanted to do was come home.'

'No problem,' Fiona said, putting the

dish into the oven. 'Just needs twenty minutes to warm through. How's your dad?'

'No change — which they tell me is a good thing. Apparently the time it takes to wake up after surgery can be variable and people tend to do it in their own time.'

Fiona nodded. She knew Becky's dad well since she and Becky had been friends since infant school. It was hard enough for her to imagine Becky's dad lying in a hospital bed still and quiet. She couldn't begin to imagine what Becky was going through.

'Well your dad does like to make an entrance. He's probably just waiting to surprise you,' Fiona said with a smile which Becky returned.

'He does like to be the life and soul of the party.' And Becky's smile turned a little watery. Fiona gave her a quick hug.

'And he will be again. He's a strong man and a fighter.'

'I know. I just wish he would wake up

and say something, even squeeze my hand.'

Fiona nodded, knowing there wasn't much more she could say.

'Wine?' she said, by way of changing the subject.

'Please.' Becky took a long sip and collapsed on to one of the kitchen chairs. 'And I'd really like to talk about something else.' Becky sighed. 'I just need to take my mind off things for a little while, you know?'

'I do,' Fiona said, adding the garlic bread to the oven before taking a seat.

'So, what have you got up to this time?'

Fiona pulled a face.

'I have got myself a bit tied up in knots if I'm honest.'

'Of course you have,' Becky said sagely but with a hint of a smile. 'Start at the beginning and don't go missing out any of your craziness. I could do with a laugh.'

They ate dinner, and Fiona was glad to see Becky eat all of hers, since she hadn't exactly been looking after herself, and then dive into the chocolate pudding that Fiona had bought.

It was only then that Fiona had finished telling Becky all about Tom.

'Wow, how do you manage to get yourself so messed up in such a short space of time?'

Fiona opened her mouth to give an indignant reply but the look on Becky's face told her that she was only joking.

'I guess I can see why you're a bit confused but I also think you might have been getting a bit ahead of yourself. I mean, it's not like he's actually asked you out or anything.'

'I know,' Fiona said, grabbing a cushion and burrowing her face in it.

'OK, well let's break it down. For starters, how do you feel about Tom?'

'Confused,' Fiona said, her voice muffled. Becky pulled the cushion from her arms.

'I got that much — but how do you feel about him?' Do you like him?'

'Yes,' Fiona said miserably.

'Well that's a good start.'

'But he kept secrets,' Fiona wailed.

'Right, two things. First is that he didn't exactly keep secrets — he just didn't tell you everything about himself in the three times you've meet him.'

'Four or five if you count the Tube station.'

Becky waved the comment away.

'And second, I hate to bring this up, Fi, but Tom is not Mark.'

'I know,' Fiona said, covering her face once more with the cushion.

'Fi, he messed you around when you were together. You can't let him continue to do that now, when you have finally moved on.'

'It seems that's easier said than done.'

Becky pulled Fiona in to a one-armed hug.

'I know and you've come so far. From what you've said this Tom guy sounds really nice and you know there are a million and one explanations for seeing him in the park with a woman, who could be family for all you know.

'Even if she is his girlfriend, you and I both know that you could do with some more friends in London. Especially since I've no idea when I might be back.'

That last comment made Fiona sit up. Here she was feeling sorry for herself when Becky was having to deal with everything going on in her life.

'I'm sorry. I've been going on and on and it's not important in the grand scheme of things.'

'Don't be daft,' Becky said, standing up. 'Coffee?' Fiona nodded. 'I need the distraction and besides I haven't stopped being your best friend.'

When Becky brought back the two cups of coffee, Fiona had a feeling that something else was going on.

'What is it?' Fiona asked. 'You know you can tell me anything.'

Becky took in a deep breath and so Fiona braced herself. She knew something big was coming.

'I've had to give notice on my flat.'

Fiona knew she looked shocked and was working hard to keep it from showing.

'I understand,' she managed to say but the words came out wobbly.

'I'm sorry . . . ' Becky started to say but Fiona waved the words away.

'You have nothing to be sorry for.'

'But when we moved to London we had a pact.'

'We did and it worked really well. I couldn't have made the move without you but there was a reason that we got separate places so that if our circumstances changed we wouldn't be leaving the other homeless or looking for a flatmate.'

'I know, but I never imagined it being like this. I do plan to come back but that is going to take time and I can't really afford to keep a flat I'm not living in.'

'Of course you can't,' Fiona said. 'It's a very sensible decision. And it's not like you really loved your flat. We can find you a better one when you are ready to come back. Maybe even think about getting one together.'

'You love your flat,' Becky said with a smile, 'but I'm sure we could find one for me — without the unreliable plumbing.'

Now they both laughed and Fiona reached for Becky's hand and gave it a squeeze.

'There is one more thing, the kind of elephant in the room.'

'If you mean the dog in the room, don't worry about it,' Fiona said, patting her lap so that Archie climbed up on to it and gave her a nose bump.

'Archie and I are getting on just fine and he's great company. Unless you want to keep him up here?' Fiona didn't really want to think about that. She loved having Archie with her, especially now he was better behaved. And there was also the Tom thing, which she quickly pushed from her mind. This wasn't about her, it was about Becky.

'I'd love to have him with me,' Becky

said with a smile that made Fiona's heart drop, 'but I spend so much time at the hospital it wouldn't be fair to him to be alone in the house all day.

'So if you can cope with him?' Becky said but there was a twinkle in her eye that told Fiona she had also guessed at the Tom connection and why Fiona might be reluctant to give Archie back right now.

'He's doing much better now we are doing some training together,' Fiona said innocently and both of them laughed with Archie barking to join in.

*   *   *

Fiona stayed a few more days but then knew she needed to get back to London. She had been able to get work done whilst Becky was visiting her dad but she had some client meetings that she couldn't put off.

'I wish I could stay longer,' Fiona said as she climbed into Becky's car to be dropped off at the station.

'I wish you could, too, but it has been amazing to have you here.'

'We'll come back soon,' Fiona promised.

'Only if you can afford it, and I mean honestly afford it,' Becky said sternly.

Fiona smiled.

'I'll look on some of those websites and see if I can get a cheap deal. I should be able to, if I book in advance. Keep me posted on how your dad is doing and you know if you need me I'll drop everything and be here.'

Becky nodded and Fiona knew her friend was fighting back tears.

'And I'll video some of Archie's training sessions so you can see how he's doing.'

Now Becky managed a smile.

'Sounds good but make sure you get the famous Tom in as well. I want to see what he looks like.'

Fiona rolled her eyes but knew that was exactly what she would do. She was excited for Becky to see Tom, too.

'Text me when you get home,' Becky

said, giving Fiona and Archie one last hug.

'I will and I'll look for those cheap tickets so we can come back soon.'

'Go, or you'll miss your train,' Becky said once more, looking like she might cry so Fiona gave her a quick tight hug and then walked away, one of the hardest things she had had to do in a long while.

Worst Fears

Fiona was trying not to check her texts every ten minutes but it was hard. On the train home she had composed a text to Tom to say that she and Archie would be back later and that she would be taking Archie for a walk around five and if Tom and Dixon were free, they would love to see them. Fiona had sent it and then reread it, wondering if she had sounded too keen.

In the end Fiona texted Becky for some advice. She got a smiley face with eyes rolled upwards and told to chill out, which she was trying to do without much luck.

At a quarter to five, Fiona gave up trying to work and clipped on Archie's lead. Even if Tom wasn't going to be there, Archie still needed a walk.

The evening was cool and they walked briskly around the lake, Archie tilting his nose in the air from time to time for a good sniff and then shrugging in disappointment.

It seemed that Archie was missing Tom and Dixon too but since Fiona had not had a reply to the text she sent saying she was going away, let alone the one she had sent to say she was back, she wasn't expecting to see either of them.

Despite telling herself all this very firmly, it wasn't just Archie that was disappointed as they headed back to the flat.

Fiona got into her pyjamas and wrapped Archie up in a blanket and they settled down for an evening in front of the TV. Fiona was glad that she had Archie with her as she knew that she would feel lonely without him but felt a pang of guilt for Becky who she knew would be going home to an empty house.

She used her phone to take a photo of her and Archie and sent it to Becky. There wasn't much she could do but she could keep in regular contact and hope that the photo made Becky smile.

Fiona had just finished her supper of toast and jam when the buzzer to the front door went. She frowned, wondering if it was worth getting up to answer it. It was obviously someone who had got the wrong flat, since she wasn't expecting anyone.

The buzzer went again and she wondered if the couple upstairs had ordered a pizza and weren't answering their own buzzer, which had happened before.

Reluctantly she walked to the buzzer. She wasn't going to the front door in her pyjamas.

'Hello? If it's pizza you've got the wrong flat.'

The speaker crackled but Fiona was sure she just heard her name.

'Who is this?' she asked, now more confused than ever.

Over the speaker there was the sound of a dog barking.

'It's Tom and Dixon.'

Fiona stared at the buzzer box, thinking she must have fallen asleep and was now dreaming.

'I know I haven't replied to your texts. I hoped to meet you in the park but I was late off of work.'

Fiona blinked. It sounded like Tom but it was also what she imagined he would do and say so it couldn't be real.

'Fiona? If now is not a good time, I can go away. I'm starting to get some funny looks out here and if anyone decides to call the police, well that could be awkward.'

Fiona laughed.

'Come on in,' she said before she could change her mind. She pulled her dressing gown around her and went to open the flat door.

'Did I get you out of bed?' Tom asked, looking horrified.

'No,' Fiona said, feeling her cheeks colour a little. 'I was cold after our walk so I thought I would put something cosy on.'

Tom stood in the hall and looked as if he might be regretting his decision to come and ring her doorbell uninvited.

'It's fine, really. Why don't you come in for a hot drink? You look frozen.'

Fiona turned and walked into her flat and Tom followed, shedding his coat and woolly hat.

'It really does seem to have taken a turn towards winter out there,' Tom said as Fiona put the kettle on.

'I guess we have been lucky so far, although I have to say Sheffield is much colder then down here.'

'How is your friend and her dad?'

'He's much the same but the hospital say that's not a bad thing. People can take a while to come round after his type of operation. Becky is hanging in there but it's not easy for her.'

Tom nodded as if he understood and Fiona indicated that he should sit down. Dixon and Archie were curled up together in Archie's bed as Fiona handed Tom a mug of hot chocolate, complete with tiny marshmallows. They both took a sip as if they weren't sure what to say.

'I hope your situation on Saturday got sorted out,' Fiona said mildly in what she hoped was an impression that she wasn't overly interested.

Tom took another sip of his hot chocolate and Fiona knew he was stalling.

'It's sorted, thanks. I'm sorry I had to run off like that.'

'No problem, I understand,' Fiona said, trying to bear in mind what Becky had said. She hadn't known Tom for that long and so couldn't expect him to share all the details of his life with her straight away.

'I'd like to make it up to you. Perhaps we could go out and eat again tomorrow after a dog training session.'

'Sounds good,' Fiona said, thinking how impressed Becky was going to be at her poise when she told her all about this later.

As soon as Tom left, Fiona video called Becky and told her all about it.

Becky looked tired but there was some good news that her dad's condition was improving and she was suitably impressed with how Fiona had behaved.

The next day, Fiona made herself focus on work and not obsess about the later meeting which she felt was good progress.

As Becky had suggested, Fiona should treat Tom as a friend and not look for anything more unless Tom gave clear signs that was what he wanted. And by clear signs, apparently Becky would only accept Tom actually saying it out loud.

When it came to getting changed to go out, Fiona didn't allow herself any time to dither over outfit choices. You didn't when you were going out to meet a friend, or at least that was Becky said.

Tom and Dixon were waiting at the spot that had become the meeting place and Fiona let out a little sigh of relief. A small part of her had wondered if Tom would not be there, perhaps being called away to work or some other excuse.

Fiona shook her head at herself — no, not an excuse, a real situation that happened to people and nothing should be read into the situation.

Fiona smiled and waved at Tom as Archie pulled on his lead and whined, wanting to get to Dixon quicker than Fiona was walking.

'Archie,' she said in a slight warning tone that Tom had taught her. Archie looked up and huffed but settled back to the steady trot that meant he kept pace with Fiona.

'Good boy,' Fiona said, feeling a little smug as she could see Tom raise a hand and give her the thumbs up.

'Afternoon!' she said cheerfully, feeling like a star pupil.

'Hi,' Tom said. 'Ready to learn some more tricks of the trade?'

'We are,' Fiona said, looking down at Archie, who she could swear was grinning up at her and she wasn't sure that was a good sign.

'Right, let's start with some off the lead recall. Are you all right with the commands?' Tom asked. Fiona nodded. Of course she was, she had practised lots of times now.

'Hang on,' Tom said just as Fiona unclipped Archie's lead. Whatever it was that Tom had seen, Archie had seen too, because all Fiona could do was stand and stare as Archie ran off into the distance.

'Call him back!' Tom yelled. 'Fiona!'

Tom's hand on her arm brought Fiona back to the here and now as she realised that she hadn't done any of the things she should have in order to prevent Archie disappearing. She had just let him go.

'Archie!' she croaked.

'Louder!' Tom said as he started to run in the direction that Archie had taken. Fiona could see it now. In the distance a few teenagers had gathered to play football and she had let Archie off the lead as the first kick of the game had started.

'Archie!' she tried to yell as she ran to catch up with Tom. Tom was easily ahead of her and she could see that he had grabbed some treats from the pouch on his belt.

'Keep calling him!' Tom shouted, sounding not even slightly out of breath which irked Fiona slightly.

'Here . . . boy . . . ' she managed between gasps.

Archie didn't even prick up his ears. He was focused on the football. The lads were focused on their game and didn't even notice Archie, until he leapt in the air and grabbed the ball in his teeth. Fiona was still some distance away but she could see that Archie's sharp little teeth had punctured the ball and it was starting to deflate.

One of the lads made a grab for Archie but he seemed to think this was part of the game and ran even further away.

Tom was close on his heels, as were a couple of the lads and Fiona could feel the all too familiar fear as she could hear the sounds of the road drawing nearer with every step.

'Archie! Stop!' she screamed, as loud as she could. Archie continued to duck away from Tom and the lads and all Fiona could see was the road ahead.

'Archie!' She was pleading now and she knew it.

There was a squeal of brakes and shouts and Fiona felt the strength go from her legs. Black dots started to dance in front of her eyes but she couldn't stop running.

'Archie!' This time it came out as a sob. She knew she would give anything to hear him bark. Any sign that he was OK.

Just Good Friends?

Fiona burst through the gap in the tall fence that ran around the edge of the park and took in the scene before her. She could see Tom speaking to one of the drivers and took in the sight that the car behind the front one had driven into the back.

No-one seemed hurt but there was obviously damage. It wasn't that she didn't care just that she needed to see what had happened to Archie. She scanned the street and spotted him.

Archie still had hold of the ball but was being held on the lead tightly by the tallest lad, who had impossibly spiky hair and oversized jeans.

'Archie? Are you OK?' Fiona asked, kneeling down and running her hands all over Archie.

'He's fine — better than our ball anyway.'

Now Fiona was satisfied, she stood up.

'I'm so sorry about that. It's my friend's dog and I had no idea he had such a thing about footballs.'

The lad sniffed.

'I'll pay for it, of course.'

The lad nodded, still unimpressed.

'It was an expensive one.'

'You can get them in the market for a fiver,' Tom said, 'and besides, you're not allowed to play football in that part of the park.'

The lad stared down at his feet and shuffled them.

'What are you, a copper or something?' he grumbled.

Fiona thought Tom was going to say that he was exactly that but he didn't, he just smiled.

'Here,' he said taking a ten pound note from his wallet. 'Go buy yourself a new ball but play down in the football pitches, all right?'

'Cheers, mate,' the lad said, handing Tom Archie's lead before running off to meet up with the rest of his team, waving the note in the air.

'What about the drivers?' Fiona said, wondering how much it was going to cost her.

'They're insured and besides I got there in time to slow them right down so there is little damage.'

'Aren't I liable? I mean I let Archie off the lead?'

'Fortunately the lady behind is a dog lover and when I explained the situation she said that her insurance company would sort it. She was just relieved that Archie was unhurt.'

Fiona shook her head.

'Are you OK?' Tom asked, sounding concerned.

'I just can't believe that you managed to sort that all out.'

Tom grinned.

'Problem solving and defusing situations is a key part of the job.'

Fiona took a deep breath as her mind started to play images of what could have happened.

'I think you need to sit down. You've gone a funny colour.'

There was a low brick wall running along the outside of the park fence and Fiona found herself guided there by Tom.

'Take some deep breaths. Everything's fine.'

Fiona tried to slow her breathing and watched as the traffic started to flow again.

'I'm so sorry. It was all my fault. I got over confident and didn't even look for any distractions.'

'I only just spotted them. And these things will happen — we just need to train Archie to ignore them.'

Archie was wrestling the ball and pawing at it and so Fiona couldn't help but think that was unlikely.

'I didn't realise footballs were his thing.'

'And I didn't realise Dixon had a thing for squirrels until he went haring after them that first time.'

'Thank you . . . I got so scared

that . . . ' Fiona couldn't talk as a lump formed in her throat. She could feel tears start to build up behind her eyes.

'Hey. It's OK,' Tom said, putting an arm around her shoulder. Fiona could think of all the reasons she shouldn't but she ignored them, turning her face into his chest and allowing Tom to hug her.

'I know it's not what you want to hear but when you've had a situation like this it is best to get straight back on the horse, so to speak.'

'You want me to let Archie off his lead again?' Fiona squeaked into Tom's jacket and she felt the rumble of a chuckle run through him.

'Yes — but this time I will make sure there are no distractions, OK?'

Fiona thought that she would agree to anything in that moment. Tom seemed to have the effect of making it seem like everything would be OK. Reluctantly, she moved away and nodded.

'Best to leave a session on a high,'

Tom said briskly, standing up.

'Where's Dixon?' Fiona said, feeling panic rise again.

'Over there,' Tom said pointing to Dixon who was sitting down just inside the park, obviously waiting for them.

'See?' Fiona said, directing her comment to Archie. 'Now that's what you're supposed to do.'

'Come on then,' Tom said, reaching out for her hand and pulling her to her feet. Tom showed no sign of wanting to let go and so Fiona walked by his side, holding on tight.

As they passed a rubbish bin Tom took the ball from Archie and placed it inside. Archie barked but soon realised that there was no way that he was getting his ball back and after a grumble fell back in beside them.

They found a quiet section of the park and Fiona and Archie practised recall, over small distances at first and then getting further away. Fiona felt some of her fear subside as Archie consistently came back when she called.

'Right — I don't know about you but I've worked up an appetite so why don't we call it a day?'

'Good idea,' Fiona said, giving Archie his last treat.

'Are you happy to go to the pub again? There aren't too many dog-friendly places around here.'

Fiona remembered the great food and roaring fire and smiled.

'Perfect,' she said.

They walked side by side across the park. Fiona wanted to reach out and hold Tom's hand again but she could hear Becky's voice in her head. No, let him make the moves, then you know it's not your imagination.

The hand-holding earlier might have just been some friendly support after a traumatic incident. Not that she planned to share all of those details with Becky. She didn't want her worrying about Archie when she had enough to deal with.

The pub was busy and the tables near the fire were taken but Tom managed to find a small table in the corner that was near enough to the radiator to feel cosy. Both the dogs settled themselves under the table. Archie seemed finally to have worn himself out.

'It's traditional pub food night,' Tom said. 'I recommend the ham, egg and chips.' He handed over the menu and Fiona scanned it before agreeing that sounded perfect. Tom went over to the bar to order and fetch their drinks.

'Feeling better?' Tom asked when he returned.

'Yes,' Fiona said, smiling ruefully. 'Sorry about that. I'm usually good in a crisis but when it's Archie I seem to fall apart.'

'Animals have a real effect on you. I work with some hard-core officers but they go all wobbly if they think something is up with their dog.'

'You mean working dogs?'

Tom chuckled.

'Never call them that in front of a dog handler.'

'Sorry,' Fiona said.

Tom laughed.

'They are, of course, but we have incredible bonds and tend to treat them like colleagues. They even have their own ID and number.'

'I guess you spend a lot of time with them?'

'Twenty-four seven. But I wouldn't want it any other way,' Tom said, leaning down to rub Dixon's belly. 'I've had Dixon since he was eight weeks old.'

'Becky's had Archie since he was a puppy too, so I guess I kind of have too.'

'You've known Becky for a while, then?'

'Since we were small,' Fiona said, smiling at the waitress who had brought them their supper.

'I've lost touch with most of my friends from when I was a kid,' Tom said. 'It's a shame, really. When you are at school you think those friendships will last for ever.'

'Becky is the only one I really keep in touch with but I know what you mean. I guess you make some strong friendships in your line of work?' Fiona didn't want to use the word police or officer, unsure if they were taboo in a public setting.

'I have, which is great, but the problem is you spend a lot of time talking about work and sometimes it's good to have a break from that.' Tom grinned at Fiona and she smiled back, doing her best not to see that as a promising sign.

'I'm sure you have other friends outside of work,' Fiona prompted, thinking of the woman in the park.

Tom frowned and Fiona thought he might have seen through her not so subtle hint.

'I do,' he said with a shrug, 'but it's complicated.'

They sat in silence for a few seconds. Fiona wasn't really sure what to say to that. To ask for more details seemed to be nosey.

'So you won the new website design job then?' Tom asked.

Fiona knew he was changing the subject but decided pressing him for more information might rock the boat again. She was enjoying Tom's company and if they were destined to just be friends then it was better than the idea of not having Tom in her life at all.

Big Disappointment

Fiona didn't think she had ever seen Becky so excited, or at least not for a long while.

'Hi, Becks! You look happy,' Fiona said, smiling at the screen around Archie who was trying to climb inside it to give Becky a hug.

'Dad's breathing on his own, Fi. It's amazing and a really important step forward.'

'That's fantastic. I told you he was a fighter,' Fiona said, throwing one arm around Archie so she could see at least part of the screen.

'Auntie Jo is coming down from Scotland to stay with me for a week, too.'

'I'm glad, some company will be good for you.'

'It's better than that, she is insisting that I take a few days away from Dad.

The doctors are saying that all the signs are good and so Auntie Jo thinks I should come to London for a few days and have a break.'

Becky was bouncing up and down like a child who just got exactly what they wanted for Christmas.

'I'm so excited. I don't want to be away too long but Jo is right, I could do with a change of scene.'

'When are you coming? I'll make up the spare room!'

They both laughed since they knew Becky would be sleeping on the sofa, no doubt with Archie.

'Auntie Jo is coming Wednesday and so I'll come Friday and if Dad is all right I'll stay till Sunday if that's OK with you?'

'Perfect!'

Becky nodded happily.

'So how is Tom?'

'Tom's good,' Fiona said mildly annoyed that her face was colouring but unable to stop the reaction.

'Uh huh. Well, I'm hoping that I will

get to see him in action.'

Fiona gave her a look.

'I mean see you and Archie showing off all you have learned. You seem to see Tom most days so I don't suppose you'll need to organise anything special. I can just come along.'

'Of course,' Fiona said, a little too eagerly. 'I mean, we are meeting for a session on Saturday afternoon.'

'Great, then we can go to that pub you are always going on about.'

'Yep. You'll love the open fire. It's like being in the countryside.'

'You may have mentioned that! Anyway, better go, I need to get up to the hospital but I'll text you when I'm on my way.'

'See you then!' Fiona said, waving at the screen until it had gone black.

'Your mummy's coming!' Fiona said to Archie who started to urgently lick her nose. 'And your grandad is getting better.'

Archie barked at this as if he understood every word, which Fiona suspected he might.

* ★ *

Fiona had worked hard and in the evenings, too, to make sure she didn't have to think about work during Becky's visit. Becky had arrived at lunchtime on Friday and they had done little more than drink tea and talk.

There seemed to be so much to catch up on, despite the fact that they had only seen each other the week before.

Fiona had told Tom that Becky was coming and asked if he minded having her come along to their session.

Tom had sounded keen and even suggested going to the pub afterwards so in Fiona's mind all was right in the world. She was really looking forward to finding out what Becky thought about Tom and whether she thought he was showing any signs of their being more than friends.

Fiona tried to act nonchalant but she knew she was failing miserably. Becky knew her too well and even a morning trip to the shops didn't seem to distract her. When it was time to head to the park, Fiona knew that Becky was watching her closely.

'Are you ready?' Fiona asked for something to say, since Becky was wearing her wellingtons and was dressed for the weather.

'I am, if you are,' Becky said with a smirk.

'Oh, stop it,' Fiona said but couldn't hide her smile.

They set out for the park and Archie was being remarkably well behaved and walking beside them on the lead without pulling at all.

'I must say Tom is a miracle worker. Archie and I went to all the puppy classes but he never seemed to grasp the basics or if he did, he wasn't keen to put them into practice.'

'All part of his job I guess and he does seem to have a natural affinity with dogs.'

'And Fionas,' Becky said and Fiona elbowed her friend playfully in the side.

'This is the spot,' Fiona said as they

reached the lake. She looked at her watch. They were a few minutes early but she had hoped that Tom and Dixon would be there waiting for them. Somehow in her head that seemed to be a less awkward way for her best friend to meet the man she fancied.

'Relax, Fi. I'm sure Tom and I will get on like a house on fire.'

Fiona nodded. She knew that they had to. She couldn't see herself dating another man that Becky wasn't keen on. Becky had not clicked with Mark, although she had worked hard to hide it and it had turned out that her reservations had been right.

Mark was not the man for Fiona and she had gone through a lot of heartache before reaching that conclusion herself.

After ten minutes, Fiona started to check her phone. There were no messages from Tom and Fiona had a sinking feeling. Surely he wasn't going to stand her up again, without sending a message.

Tom not being able to make it she

could cope with but this, especially when he knew that she was bringing Becky along to meet him, was more than she thought she could bear.

After another few minutes standing in silence, with Becky shifting from foot to foot with the cold seeping up from the ground, Fiona knew she had to do something.

'Why don't we go to the café and warm up? I'll text Tom and tell him that's where we are, so he can meet us there.'

'Good idea,' Becky said but Fiona recognised the overly enthusiastic tone. It was a tone that told Fiona that Becky knew she was disappointed.

They drank their hot chocolate slowly and talked about other things, or at least Becky did, which Fiona was grateful for.

Anything to distract her from the reality that Tom had stood them both up and hadn't even bothered to let them know he couldn't make it.

And this time was worse than the

last. This time she had Becky with her and this made it more mortifying.

'I don't think he's coming,' Fiona said, checking her phone one last time. 'Let's walk Archie around the lake and head home.'

Becky reached out for Fiona's hand and gave it a squeeze.

'Maybe he got caught up at work. He has the kind of job for it.'

Fiona nodded. This was true but it still didn't explain why he hadn't let her know. Surely he could take thirty seconds to send her a simple text. But he hadn't and it reminded her so much of the way Mark had treated her that she was in danger of breaking down in tears.

They stepped outside and Becky put her arm through Fiona's.

'Let's get a takeaway and get into our PJs. We can watch whatever cheesy movie you pick.'

They walked off together arm in arm, with Archie behaving himself and Fiona was glad that Becky was with her.

Somehow Becky had the power to make it feel like things were going to be all right, even if it didn't look like it right now.

'OK, but nothing romantic,' Fiona said, trying to focus on the fact that she had some precious time with Becky and didn't want to spend it moping over a man who couldn't even be bothered to text her to let her know his plans had changed.

'Action comedies it is, then,' Becky said triumphantly and now Fiona did manage a laugh. Becky was famous for hating anything romantic, much preferring movies that made her laugh.

★ ★ ★

Sunday came round quicker than Fiona thought was possible, as it always did when there was something you were dreading. Becky was going back to Sheffield and Fiona was going to miss her. They had avoided the subject of Tom all Saturday evening and Sunday

155

morning but now Becky was packing her bags and Fiona doubted her friend would leave without bringing up the subject.

'OK,' Becky said, glancing at her watch, 'time for one last quick pep talk.'

Fiona rolled her eyes and made a show of groaning although in reality she felt like she needed someone to tell her what to do next, since she had no idea, despite the fact that she had thought about little else.

'You like Tom, yes?'

'I liked Mark,' Fiona said miserably, 'and look how well that turned out.'

'Fi, Tom is not Mark,' Becky said sharply before giving her friend a quick squeeze.

'I think you need to give Tom an opportunity to explain. He might have a really good reason and it would be a shame not to give him a chance.'

Fiona shrugged. Part of her wanted to do that and the other part thought that she needed to protect herself from the kind of heartache that Mark had brought into her life.

'You give him one chance and if you need to, you ask him outright. If he gives you an answer, one that you can live with, then you keep seeing him. If not, then you have to think about whether you want someone like that in your life.'

Despite everything, Fiona just wanted Tom to explain, to have a really good reason, then they could continue to be friends and maybe explore something more. The last time she had seen Tom, she had been sure that he wanted that too but now, now she wasn't so sure.

At the train station, they both had to fight back tears. Having Becky to stay had felt like a glimmer of how life had been and now it was time to face reality once more.

They gave each other tight hugs and Becky hugged and kissed Archie, telling him to be a good boy, before she got on her train and made her way back up north.

One thing they hadn't discussed,

Fiona thought, as she and Archie walked slowly home was whether Fiona should be the one to make the first move.

Should she text him to ask why he hadn't met up with them as promised or should she wait and see whether Tom texted her? Maybe Becky was right and something had happened to Tom at work.

That thought was enough to make up Fiona's mind. Over the last 24 hours her thoughts about Tom hadn't been that charitable but now she faced that reality, she knew that she needed to be the one to make the first move.

Hurrying along, she and Archie made it back home in record time. Only pausing long enough to pull off her gloves, she sent Tom a text.

'Hi, Tom. We missed you yesterday. I hope everything is OK with you and Dixon. Fiona x'.

Fiona pressed Send before she could reread the text. She knew if she did she would procrastinate over sending it and most likely never actually press the button.

Now all she could do was wait, and she decided that catching up on some work would be the most useful distraction.

Fiona's phone pinged just as she emailed her latest website design to her new clients. She was proud of the work and confident that they would love it, too. It had been a good distraction from thinking — no, worrying — about what might have happened to Tom.

She picked up her phone and saw immediately that it wasn't Tom. It was a message from Becky to say that she was home safe and off to the hospital to see her dad. Fiona was pleased, of course she was, but she had hoped that it would be a message from Tom.

The more time that passed the more her imagination started to run wild.

Feeble Explanations

Curled up on the sofa under her duvet with Archie as her hot water bottle, Fiona tried to focus on the evening's TV but all she could do was fret. What if something had happened to Tom at work?

She had even checked the local news website to see if anything had made the news but there was nothing. Fiona knew this was a good thing but it did nothing to calm her worries.

When her phone pinged, she jumped but it was only another message from Becky.

'Has he texted you yet?'

Fiona typed back, 'No' with a sad face.

'Maybe you should, you know, ring him?'

Fiona stared at the phone. Somehow that hadn't really occurred to her.

'Don't you think that would give the wrong impression?'

'What? That he didn't turn up when he was supposed to and you are concerned??????' The row of question marks seemed to go on for ever.

'RING HIM!'

Fiona sighed and knew that she wouldn't get away without doing it. Becky would just keep bombarding her with texts and phone calls till she did.

'Fine. Ringing him now,' Fiona sent back.

After the first few rings, Fiona was sure that Tom wouldn't answer and was just composing the message she would leave on his answer machine, when the phone clicked.

'Hello?' the person said, but Fiona knew it wasn't Tom's voice. For starters, it was female. There was a lot of noise in the background, shouts and the sounds of things being thrown around.

'Hello?' the woman at the other end of the phone said and she sounded distracted. Fiona wasn't at all surprised since it sounded like she was standing near to a small riot.

'I'm sorry I must have the wrong number,' Fiona started to say but she knew this couldn't be true since she had had phone calls and texts from this number from Tom. 'Sorry — is Tom there?' she added eventually.

'He's busy,' the woman said, 'and if this is work, don't be expecting him in. He's done enough overtime lately.'

'Er . . . ' Fiona didn't know what to say to that. 'Bye then,' she said but she doubted the woman at the other end had heard her, as the phone line went dead.

All Fiona could do for several minutes was stare at the phone and try to make sense of what had just happened but she couldn't seem to find any order to her thoughts.

When her phone rang, it made her jump but thankfully it was Becky. If Tom had rung in that moment she didn't think she would have been able to speak to him.

'Well? What did he say?'

'He didn't answer,' Fiona said blankly.

'Oh, did you leave a message?'

'No.'

'Fi, you need to ring back and leave one.'

'I couldn't leave a message because a woman answered the phone.'

There was silence from the other end.

'Well, maybe it was his mum or his sister?'

'Maybe.'

'Oh, Fi, I'm sorry — I should never have encouraged you.'

'It's fine. It's not like we ever talked about whether we had partners or anything.'

'Well, if he had one, he should have said,' Becky said, sounding cross, but Fiona knew it was just because she was fiercely protective.

'No, he shouldn't. He was just helping me out with Archie. It's not like he has done anything wrong.'

'Fiona, I know what I said earlier about Tom not being Mark but you are starting to sound just like you did when you were with Mark. Don't make excuses for him.'

'I'm not, Becky, really but I do feel like I should give him a chance to explain himself.'

Fiona sighed. She knew that Becky was probably right. She had worked hard to get her life back on track and to be happy, was she ready to risk all that for another complicated relationship?

'OK, let's talk about something else,' Becky said and Fiona smiled that her friend knew her so well.

★ ★ ★

Monday and Tuesday came and went and Fiona knew that she needed to put all thoughts of Tom aside. She was never going to understand what had happened but now that she knew he hadn't been hurt at work, she needed to stop worrying and move on with her life.

164

She had even started taking Archie for a long walk first thing in the morning before she started work as she didn't want to risk bumping into Tom.

Wednesday morning was wet and cold but since it didn't seem to be getting better Fiona thought they should brave it anyway. Even Archie didn't make a fuss when she put his coat on. They trotted off to the park and did a half circuit of the lake before turning around and heading for home. Archie was wet and muddy despite his coat and even he didn't have the enthusiasm for it today.

Walking home into the wind, Fiona had her head down against the rain. Archie trotted beside her but suddenly lurched forward. Fiona increased her grip on his lead.

'Steady, Archie. Today is not a day to run off.'

But still Archie pulled on his lead. Fiona looked up and saw the reason walking towards her, with his hat pulled down to shield his eyes. Briefly Fiona thought about crossing back over the road but Archie starting barking before she could take any action.

'Fiona! There you are. I've been looking for you.'

Fiona just stared. She hadn't heard from him for four days, not even a text and now he was making a big deal about looking for her.

'I've been where I usually am, at home,' Fiona said, wishing she could keep some of the hurt from her tone.

'I know. I'm sorry, today has been my first chance to come over and see you.'

Fiona raised an eyebrow — did he really expect her to believe that? Tom took in her expression and nodded as if he understood, which somehow made Fiona feel more cross than she had before.

'Look can we go for a drink, get out of the weather?'

Fiona knew it would be polite to ask him to her place, which was not far away but she wasn't sure she wanted to. Neutral territory seemed a better plan, one that she could leave whenever she wanted to.

'Sure,' Fiona said and turned away from her flat. If Tom was surprised, he said nothing and they walked together in silence.

Even Archie seemed to pick up on the vibes that something was off and so trotted beside them without making his usual song and dance.

By the time they reached the pub, Fiona was soaked through and all she wanted to do was go home and get changed into something warm. But she had come this far, she should at least give Tom a few minutes to explain himself.

Not that she thought he would be able to come up with anything that would convince her they could be friends, but still . . .

The pub was quiet as it was after the lunchtime rush and so they were able to get seats by the fire. Both dogs sat as close as they could and the rain seemed to steam off them.

'Hot drinks, I think?' Tom suggested. Fiona nodded. 'I'll get sandwiches, too,' he added and Fiona shrugged as if to say it didn't matter to her one way or the other.

She shook herself. She knew she was being childish. It wasn't as if they had been dating and if she claimed to be Tom's friend then she needed to give him a chance to explain, without her making it worse with her attitude.

Tom came back with two mugs of hot chocolate and passed one to Fiona. She wrapped her hands around it and looked up at Tom, trying for an encouraging smile.

'Right,' Tom said, 'I know I have a lot of explaining to do.'

Fiona nodded and gave a wry smile — that much they could agree on.

Tom took a deep breath and started to speak.

'Well, my job makes lots of demands on me.'

Fiona nodded again, that much she had figured out herself. She just didn't

168

understand why Tom's job meant he was unable to send a text.

'I get called upon even when I'm off duty and often at the last minute. It's one of the issues with having a dog as good as Dixon.'

Fiona smiled. Dixon was certainly well behaved and she could imagine he was good at what he did, sniffing out things that criminals shouldn't have but then she remembered how he had reacted to her at the Tube station and her smile shifted a little.

'He does, however, have the odd lapse, as you have experienced, but all I can say to that is I'm sorry but Dixon is in love with you.'

Fiona now laughed and Tom joined her. Fiona felt some of the uncertainty fade away. Moments like these were why she had come to like Tom and feel more for him but she knew she still needed to get to the bottom of all this.

'I understand, Tom, really I do, and I respect your job.'

Tom looked relieved and Fiona was a little surprised.

'What?' Fiona asked curiously.

'Let's just say that not all my friends are that understanding.'

'Well, I imagine they do wonder why you can't send a simple text to let them know your plans had changed.' Fiona raised an eyebrow and she knew she was laying out a challenge.

Either Tom explained himself in a way she could live with or she wasn't sure their friendship, or anything more, had a future.

Tom at least looked sheepish.

'Yes, about that . . . '

Tom paused and Fiona wondered if he expected her to step in and say that it was fine, that she understood but in reality she didn't understand and she wanted to, so she said nothing.

'Right,' Tom said realising that Fiona wasn't going to help him out. 'The first time, I completely forgot.'

Fiona nodded, that wasn't great news but she could live with it as a one off.

'OK . . . ' she said, waiting for him to explain the last time which was much more important.

'The second time, I kind of lost my phone and that was the only place I had your number, which is why I had to come and track you down in person.'

Fiona nodded again but inside her mind was racing. Had he lost his phone? If he had, who was the woman who answered and why did she say Tom was busy?

Their food arrived and they started to eat. Fiona couldn't think of anything to say and so for the first few minutes they ate in silence.

'I hope you understand and I promise not to let it happen again.' Tom pulled a phone from his pocket. 'I have a new phone and everything.'

'OK,' she found herself saying and smiling. But it wasn't OK. Tom was lying to her and she couldn't figure out why.

Tom changed the subject and they talked about other things, Fiona trying her best to behave normally.

At the end of the meal, Tom asked her for her phone number and she gave it to him. They hugged goodbye outside the pub but this time Tom didn't offer to walk her home and she knew he must have picked up on the fact that something was a little off between them but she couldn't worry about that at the moment.

Right now she needed to try and figure out why Tom was lying and what it might mean for their future. He hadn't mentioned seeing her in the park, when he was with another woman. Maybe he hadn't realised it was her. He had certainly seemed distracted.

But to Fiona, it felt like the lies, or at best, half-truths, were starting to pile up. And Fiona wasn't sure that was something she could cope with, even if they were just friends.

Shattered Dreams

'He told you he lost his phone?' Becky's voice was incredulous and it matched the expression on her face, a cross between exasperation and concern for her friend.

'That's what he said.'

'So he clearly doesn't know that you rang him and some woman answered?'

'Apparently not.'

'I suppose it could be whoever found or stole his phone?'

'Then why did she say that he was busy and that if it was work he had done enough overtime?' Fiona said miserably.

'Oh, Fi, you know if I was there I would be round in a shot with double choc chip ice-cream and a bottle of wine.'

'I know you would,' Fiona said, managing a smile. 'I think I know what

I need to do now.'

Becky said nothing, waiting for Fiona to continue as Archie shuffled on to Fiona's lap and gave her nose a quick comforting lick. Fiona smiled at him and stroked his fur.

'I think I need to just see him as a person who has offered to help with Archie but after the next session I think I need to put an end to it.'

Becky nodded thoughtfully.

'Or you could ask him outright about the woman who answered his phone and the woman in the park.'

Fiona shook her head.

'I can't do that. I mean he has never made any overt signs that he wanted anything more with me, and so it's not like he has done anything wrong.

'As you said, he is entitled to a private life and he doesn't have to share everything with me. I'm just the woman he met in the park who he is doing a favour.'

Becky looked at Fiona and Fiona knew what was coming next.

'All that was true ... in the beginning but meeting up with your best friend, buying you dinner and all that and then lying to you, Fi, he does owe you.' Becky held up a hand to still Fiona's reply. 'Not everything but at least the truth about that. Even if you are just friends, he still lied.'

Fiona sighed. Becky was probably right but she just couldn't see herself confronting Tom about it. She was no good at that sort of thing, mostly opting for the path of least resistance.

'Or ... ' Becky said and there was that glint in her eye which Fiona knew meant trouble. 'Or you could give me Tom's old phone number and I could ring it and see what I can find out about this woman.'

Fiona's eyes went wide. She thought she was used to Becky's crazy ideas but this seemed to top them.

'You can't do that!' Fiona said.

'Why not? I won't say who I am. I'll just see what I can find out and then at least you will know.'

'I'm not sure . . . ' Fiona said.

'Fi, you might be throwing away a perfectly good friendship that has the possibility of being much more. And it's not like Tom will ever find out, will he?'

Fiona nodded.

'Text me his old number now, before you chicken out.'

Fiona glared at her friend and sent the text, knowing that Becky knew exactly how to get her to do something she wasn't sure about.

'I'll call you back when I've got through,' Becky said and Fiona's screen went blank as Becky hung up.

Fiona paced up and down as Archie sat on the sofa and watched. Why had she let Becky goad her into it? She should have taken some time to think about it.

When her phone beeped to say that Becky wanted to video chat, Fiona pounced on it. There wasn't anything she could do now, except find out what Becky had found out.

'Well?' Fiona said.

Becky raised an eyebrow but Fiona wasn't about to apologise for the mess that Becky had likely got her into.

'Relax, Fi, I know how to do this sort of thing.'

Fiona tried to take a deep breath but failed.

'Just tell me.'

'It was a woman who answered the phone and I pretended to be a colleague from work.'

Fiona groaned. What if this woman knew all Tom's friends from work?

'She believed me, Fi, relax. Anyway, she said that Tom had lent her his phone as hers had been broken. I said Tom was that kind of friend and she said he was family.'

Fiona stared at the screen. Tom had a partner or a wife. She should have known.

'Fi, she could have been any kind of family member, it doesn't mean there is anything romantic between them.

'I mean, if someone rang you and asked you about your boyfriend or husband you would say that was your relationship. You wouldn't say they were family.' Becky was sounding triumphant now and Fiona could feel herself relax a little.

'But it still doesn't explain why he wouldn't just come out and say it.'

Becky nodded.

'But there could be any number of reasons, Fi, and they aren't all bad. I think you should keep meeting up with him for dog training and he'll probably open up.

'You could try talking about your family, that's the best way to get someone else talking.'

Perhaps Becky was right. What harm could it do to spend a bit more time with Tom? If they had established that Tom didn't have a girlfriend or a wife then she didn't need to feel guilty about her feelings putting Tom in a difficult spot.

'Well?' Becky said with a wry smile and Fiona realised that she had been waiting for Fiona to say something.

'Sorry, just thinking.'

Becky laughed — she knew Fiona too well.

'And?' Becky prompted.

'And I think you might be right. I'll keep doing the dog training with him and see what happens.'

'Perfect, and don't let the distance make you forget that I'm always right!'

'As if you would ever let me!' Fiona grinned at her friend and they said their goodbyes.

Tom and Fiona had arranged to meet the next day in the morning as Tom had to work the late shift. Fiona had it all straight in her mind. She wasn't going to obsess over the missing phone or the lie. There was likely to be a perfectly logical explanation, just as Becky had said.

Family matters were complicated and she knew herself that you didn't always want to share all the details with people you had just met.

Fiona and Archie headed to the park early. Fiona wanted to have some time to practise with Archie. She ignored the voice in her head that told her she was trying to impress Tom and focused on getting Archie to sit, stay and come back when she let him off the lead.

As if he knew how important it all was, Archie behaved perfectly. Archie was sitting beside her, waiting to be told the command to go, when Tom appeared in the distance.

At least Fiona thought it was Tom, since he didn't have his usual shadow at his side. There was no sign of Dixon. Fiona felt a stab of concern. Archie started to run in Tom's direction and Fiona let him as she hurried along behind him.

'Tom,' she said, slightly out of breath, as Tom made a fuss of Archie, 'is everything OK? Where's Dixon?'

Tom stood up and his face said everything. Something was wrong, very wrong.

'What is it?' Fiona said reaching a hand for his arm. Tom stared at the hand and Fiona quickly withdrew as she tried to work out what was happening.

'I didn't bring him because I knew I wouldn't be here very long.'

'Oh,' Fiona said, 'do you have to work?' The question gave her a glimmer of hope but it faded quickly with the look on Tom's face.

'No, not till later.'

'Right,' Fiona said, feeling adrift at what was happening.

'I came to tell you that I won't be able to help you with Archie's training any more.'

'Right,' Fiona said again. 'You're busy, I understand,' she added.

Tom nodded and it looked as if he was going to turn away and just leave.

'Tom . . . ' Fiona started to say but she had no idea what words should come next.

'Why did you ring up pretending to be someone else? That's the bit I really can't wrap my head around. I told you I'd lost my phone, why would you ring it?'

Fiona felt like she had swallowed a bucket of ice.

'I'm sorry, I was just curious . . . ' Fiona didn't think now was the time to tell him that it was actually Becky who rang his phone. Somehow it seemed like that would make things worse, if that was possible.

'Curious about what? I explained what happened.'

'But you didn't really,' Fiona started to say but Tom cut her off.

'What you mean is I didn't tell you something you were happy with so, what? You decided to check up on me?'

Fiona wanted to say that she had rung his phone before his explanation. That she had spoken to a woman and that was why she had, or Becky had, rung it again.

Perhaps if he knew he had been caught out in a lie, or at least a half truth then he might be less angry. But Tom didn't give her the chance.

'I don't need this drama in my life right now, Fiona. I liked you, I thought we could even . . . ' He didn't finish his sentence, just turned on his heel and walked away.

Fiona watched him go. She didn't think she could move even if she had wanted to. Her legs felt like lead as did the rest of her.

Her mind kept replaying what had just happened and coming up with the things that she should have said but didn't. Archie whined at her side and she could see that he was shivering.

'Sorry, boy. Let's go home and get warm. There's nothing more that we can do here.'

They turned for home and even Archie seemed subdued.

Out of the Blue

'So you haven't seen or heard from Tom in over a month?' Becky said as she and Fiona walked down the street, laden down with bags of their Christmas shopping. Becky had been able to get away for another precious weekend. Her dad was doing better, out of intensive care and on a rehabilitation ward and he had insisted that Becky have a weekend away to relax and see Fiona and Archie.

'No,' Fiona said. They had managed to avoid the conversation of Tom for the first whole day of Becky's visit and Fiona had hoped that would continue. She hadn't seen Tom, by design, she had been taking Archie to a different park for his daily constitutional.

It was further away but at least Fiona could be fairly sure that she wasn't at risk of bumping into Tom, or seeing him in the distance. She had decided that the only thing she could do was put everything that had happened with Tom behind her and get on with the rest of her life.

'You mean you haven't even seen him at the park?'

Fiona shook her head.

'Archie and I have been going to Ebben for a change of scene.'

Becky raised an eyebrow and Fiona sighed, knowing that she hadn't fooled her friend.

'I don't want to see him, Becks, and I know for a fact that he doesn't want to see me. It's better this way for both of us.'

'Uh huh,' Becky said.

'What?'

'Nothing — just wondering if he is still moping about like you are.'

Now it was Fiona's turn to give her friend a stern look.

'Look, I know I've said it before but I really am sorry about the phone call thing. Why don't you let me call him and explain it?'

'No!' Fiona said so loudly that a couple walking past stared at her and then hurried on. 'No, we talked about this. It's done, Becky, and it's fine. It's not your fault. He might be angry about what we did but he was the one lying.'

'But he might have a reasonable explanation . . . ' Becky started to say.

'He lied. I can't think what explanation that he could come up with that could cover it all and besides you didn't see him. He was angry, properly angry and I don't need that in my life.'

'Well, we've said it before and I will say it again. We have each other.'

Now Fiona did laugh, since the first time Becky had said that, was when Joey Porter had broken her heart at the tender age of eight by refusing to marry her.

'We do.'

'And I should be able to come down

more often now that Dad is doing so much better.'

'I'd like that. I do miss you, Becks.'

'Well, Dad has a rehab plan now. So we are working towards getting him home. Once he is home and getting his life back on track then I plan to come back.'

Fiona didn't say anything. She wasn't sure that she could ever see Becky feeling as though she could leave her dad. He had plenty of friends, that was true, but no family nearby and Sheffield was a long way to go in an emergency.

Living in London alone had never been the plan for Fiona and after all the stuff with Tom, Fiona had been thinking about whether she wanted to stay herself.

'Penny for 'em?' Becky asked but Fiona knew that she couldn't voice her thoughts out loud. Right now, it seemed that Becky needed to believe that she would be coming back to London to pick up her dream, and Fiona didn't want to shatter that by voicing her own doubts.

'Just thinking about Christmas. I'm off to my folks but I was thinking I could bring Archie up to you for New Year?'

'Are you sure? New Year is a big deal for your folks.'

Fiona nodded. Her parents now lived in Scotland and fully embraced Hogmanay.

'They do but they are having a massive party with friends and beside I've already said I'll be at yours and they completely understand.'

'Well, it is on the way home,' Becky said with a grin.

'Exactly,' Fiona said, smiling back. Christmas was just the distraction she needed this year and maybe the New Year would help her to move on from the hurt and disappointment.

★   ★   ★

It was lunchtime on New Year's Day when Becky finally got out of bed. It was clear to Fiona that Becky was

188

exhausted from all her responsibilities and so Fiona had let her sleep. They had seen in the New Year and then retired. Fiona had got up to take Archie for a walk and was now sitting on the sofa at Becky's dad's house, watching TV.

'What time is it?' Becky asked with a yawn, running a hand through her bed hair.

'Let's just say you've missed the morning completely.'

Becky squinted at the clock on the mantelpiece.

'I'm supposed to be at the hospital!' She said sounding panicked.

'No, you're not. Your dad said we weren't to come in until tea time, remember?'

Becky collapsed on the sofa and frowned, clearly trying to remember.

'Coffee and a bacon butty?' Fiona asked and Becky nodded.

'I can't remember the last time I slept that late.'

'Well, you must have needed it.

Archie and I have been out for a walk and washed up so all you need to do is relax.'

'I could get used to this,' Becky said with a smile, 'and I do wonder when I come back to London whether we should get a flat for the pair of us.'

'Good plan,' Fiona said in what she hoped was a non-committal, but enthusiastic voice.

'I know, I know . . . you don't want to lose your garden but I'm sure we can find somewhere bigger with a garden and then you can see Archie every day. He'll miss you if you don't,' Becky said.

Archie was on her lap and looking at Fiona as Becky lifted up his ears in what she clearly thought was a begging expression.

Fiona couldn't help laughing.

'You're right — I would miss Archie,' Fiona said, ducking the cushion that Becky threw in her direction.

There was a ringing noise.

'Your phone, Becks.'

Becky picked up her phone.

'Not me, must be yours.'

'Seems early for Mum and Dad . . . Could you have a look?' Fiona said, using her tomato-sauce-covered knife to point in the direction of her phone which was on the coffee table.

'You're not going to believe this,' Becky said picking up Fiona's phone.

'Is it Ryan Gosling ringing to ask me why I stood him up last night?' Fiona said carrying the tray of coffee and bacon butties into the lounge.

'It's Tom,' Becky said.

'Not funny,' Fiona said, giving her friend a look that made it clear she was not ready for Tom jokes just yet.

'No — really,' Becky said as Fiona put the tray down. Becky handed her the phone and Fiona could see that it was in fact Tom, or at least Tom's new number calling her.

'What should I do?' Fiona asked.

'Answer it!' Becky said. 'Quickly — before it rings off.'

The call cut out as Fiona's message service cut in. Becky stared at Fiona and Fiona stared back.

'Why is he ringing now? After all this time?' Fiona shook her head. 'It's probably just a mistake. Maybe his phone is in his pocket . . . '

'Why don't you listen to your message and find out?' Becky said. 'If he didn't mean to call there won't be a message and if he did . . . ' Becky shrugged.

Fiona's hand shook a little as she logged into her message service.

'Fiona, I'm sorry . . . I know I have no right to call after all this time and with everything that happened.

'It's just that . . . something has happened to Dixon . . . and I know you understand . . . I'm sorry — I shouldn't have called.' Then he hung up.

Fiona could feel tears in her eyes. Something had happened to Dixon and Tom sounded terrible, worse than terrible. Fiona had a flashback to the day she had lost Archie and how she had felt when she thought he had had an accident and she knew that it didn't matter what else had happened.

'Well?' Becky said and she looked worried, no doubt taking in the look on Fiona's face. Fiona handed over her phone so that Becky could listen to the message.

'That's awful,' Becky said, 'and Tom sounds in a bad way.'

Fiona nodded. She had already made up her mind. She just needed to tell Becky.

'Go,' Becky said and Fiona felt a brief sense of relief that her friend understood.

'Go. He needs you and I know you well enough to know that you can't leave a friend alone and in pain. Go.'

'But we've hardly spent any time together.'

'You can come back when, well, when Tom is OK.'

It was clear to Fiona that Becky didn't want to say out loud what might have happened to Dixon. As a dog owner, Becky knew that pain and fear of something bad happening to Archie.

193

Fiona took her phone back and dialled Tom's number. It went straight to answer phone.

'Tom, it's Fiona. I'm sorry I didn't get to the phone in time. Ring me or text me where you are and I will be there. I'm in Sheffield so I'll be there as soon as I can.'

She hung up and picked up her bag, suddenly realising that there was one person she hadn't thought about — Archie.

'It's fine,' Becky said, reading her thoughts. 'Archie can stay with me. It's not like I'm needed at the hospital twenty-four seven like I was. Now come on, or you'll miss the next train.'

On the journey back to London, all Fiona could do was grip her phone and check for messages every few minutes. Silence from Tom didn't seem like it could be good news and all she wanted to do is get there, so that he wasn't alone with dealing with whatever he was dealing with. Just as the train pulled in to Kings Cross, Fiona's phone beeped.

'Newman's Advance Veterinary Practice, Chesle Street. SW1.'

Fiona read the message several times looking for some hint as to what had happened but knew it was hopeless. So instead she opened the map app on her phone and worked out where the vet's was.

Outside the station, knowing it was New Year's Day and the bus services were limited, she hailed a black cab.

She was charged double rate but Fiona didn't care. The cab had got her there much faster than the bus would have. She paid the driver and jumped out, running to the front door of the vet's.

It was closed and there was no sign of anyone and so Fiona rang the doorbell. A nurse in green scrubs came to the door and opened it.

'Can I help you?' she asked, scanning Fiona and working out that she didn't have a pet with her in need of emergency care.

'My friend called me and asked me

to come. His name is Tom and his dog is Dixon.'

'The police officer?' she asked. Fiona nodded as the nurse, whose name badge read *Sandy,* stood back and let her in.

'Tom is in our private waiting room,' Sandy said as she led Fiona down a corridor.

'How is Dixon?' Fiona asked.

'He's in surgery. It's touch and go, I'm afraid,' Sandy said and she looked genuinely sorry. Fiona tried to swallow back the tears. She needed to be strong for Tom.

Sandy knocked gently on the door but didn't wait for a reply, merely pushed it open. And that was when Fiona saw Tom, for the first time in several months. He was sitting on the edge of his seat, in full uniform, with his head in his hands.

'Tom?' Fiona said, her voice wobbling as Sandy closed the door quietly behind her.

Tom looked up and Fiona didn't

think she had ever seen someone so heartbroken. Fiona crossed the short distance between them and pulled Tom into her arms.

Eventually he broke away and wiped his arm across his face.

'Sorry,' he said, sniffing and looking like he was making an effort to compose himself.

'You don't need to be sorry about anything,' Fiona said, holding his hand and giving it a squeeze before taking the seat beside him. 'You know I understand.'

'I can't believe you came all the way back from Sheffield just because I called.'

'You would have done the same for me,' Fiona said, hoping that was true.

Tom looked her full in the face for the first time.

'I would,' he said, squeezing her hand back. Tom was about to say something else but the door opened and he leapt to his feet, Fiona by his side.

'Dixon is stable,' the female vet said

with a tired smile. 'We've managed to stop the internal bleeding and his blood pressure has come back up to a normal range.'

'And his leg?' Tom asked.

'Dixon has had a lot to deal with and so we have decided to leave the leg for now. His body needs time to recover from the shock. In a day or two if he continues to improve we can look to see what we can do.'

'Do you think he will lose it?' Tom said and Fiona put her arm around his waist and pulled him tight.

'One thing at a time,' the vet said kindly. 'I know that he is a working dog but the most important thing right now is that he is stable.'

Tom nodded.

'Of course, thank you.' He held out his hand and the vet shook it.

'He's still very sleepy but you can come and see him if you like.'

Tom followed the vet and Fiona stayed where she was. She figured that Tom needed to do this on his own.

'Will you come with me?' Tom asked and his expression made her want to pull him into her arms and never let him go. But instead she reached for his hand and together they followed the vet to the intensive care unit.

Dixon was lying wrapped in a blanket, one leg heavily bandaged and with an IV drip. He seemed to recognise Tom immediately as his tail started to wag just a little.

'It's good to see you, boy. You had me worried there for a while.'

Dixon tried to lift up his head but Tom leaned over him so he didn't have to and Dixon licked him on the nose.

'You get some rest, buddy. I'll be back in the morning, I promise.'

Dixon whined but closed his eyes and Fiona was sure that he was losing the battle with the need to sleep. Tom stepped back and turned to the vet.

'You have my number, if anything changes, anything at all, please call me.'

'We will,' the vet said. 'Come back for eight in the morning, you can see him then and we'll have a better idea of what else we need to do.'

'Thank you,' Tom said, hugging the vet. The vet seemed quite used to being hugged by grateful owners and gave Tom a pat on the back.

'Go and get some rest,' she said as Sandy reappeared and walked them back to the front door.

'Thanks,' Tom said to her as he and Fiona stepped outside.

'Right, let's go back to mine, we'll get you warmed up and some food inside you,' Fiona said.

Tom nodded but looked reluctant to leave.

'Thanks. I don't think I could face going back to mine, without Dixon it's . . . ' In Fiona's eyes he looked ready to collapse.

'We'll find a taxi and then you can tell me all about it — or not,' she said. 'Whatever you need, I'm here.'

Lost Without You

Fiona found an oversized jumper that she kept for chilling out at home and some thick socks she wore for hiking, but none of her jogging bottoms would fit Tom so he kept his work trousers on. Whilst he got changed, Fiona made coffee and called for a pizza delivery.

Tom emerged from the bathroom in his rather unusual outfit but looking more relaxed. Fiona handed him a mug of coffee.

'Pizza will be here in twenty minutes,' she said with a smile. They made their way to the sofa and sat down.

It was strange being in the flat without Archie and so Fiona could only imagine how Tom must feel without Dixon. She pulled the throw off the back of the sofa and covered them both with it.

'Thank you,' Tom said.

'I think we've covered that,' Fiona said with a smile. 'You don't need to thank me.'

'I do, especially after our last meeting. I wouldn't have blamed you for just ignoring my call.'

Fiona looked at Tom and could see how exhausted he was.

'We don't need to talk about that now.' Tom opened his mouth to speak but Fiona held up her hand. 'We do need to talk but we can do that later, can't we? I think you've had enough to deal with right now.'

Tom seemed to relax a little.

'Do you want to tell me what happened today?' Fiona asked gently.

'It was just a normal shift. Dixon was happy to be at work and I was happy to be doing my bit to catch the bad guys.'

Fiona slipped her arm through Tom's and he looked at her gratefully.

'It all happened so fast. We were in this warehouse, sniffing out for money and contraband. The floor gave way and Dixon was ahead of me. I tried to grab him . . . ' Tom's voice was shaking and it wasn't long before the rest of him joined in.

Fiona shifted so that she could pull him into her arms and hold him tight.

'I'm so, so sorry.'

'I should have seen it, I should have checked,' Tom said fiercely.

'You're not psychic, Tom. This was not your fault.'

Tom shook his head.

'It was.'

'And when Archie ran off and nearly got hit by a car, did you tell me it was my fault?'

Tom said nothing.

'I'm telling you, Tom, and you need to hear me. I have never seen anyone care for their dog like you care for Dixon and I know that you would do anything to keep him safe but sometimes things happen outside our control.'

Tom looked at her and she wiped away the tear that had appeared on his cheek.

'I love that dog,' Tom said with a

shaky almost laugh. 'Not many people get that.'

'I do,' Fiona reassured him. 'Archie isn't even my dog and yet he feels like family.'

'Dixon's my best mate as well, you know?'

Fiona nodded.

'And he's going to be OK.'

'What about his leg? If he loses it I don't think I could forgive myself.'

'You heard the vet — one thing at a time. The most important thing is that he recovers from the surgery. We can deal with what comes next together.'

Fiona could feel Tom studying her.

'I don't deserve you,' he said softly.

'I feel the same about you,' Fiona replied and Tom leaned in and kissed her gently on the lips.

The ring of the doorbell made them break apart from their kiss.

'Pizza,' Fiona said.

Tom seemed reluctant to let her go.

'You need to eat,' Fiona said. It was only her concern for Tom's well-being that was giving her the strength to pull away herself.

Fiona padded to the door with her purse, paid for the pizza and returned to the sofa. Tom had taken a couple of beers from Fiona's fridge. They sat in silence whilst they ate, each lost in their own thoughts.

'Where is Archie?' Tom asked as if it had suddenly occurred to him.

'I left him with Becky. Her dad is doing much better so she doesn't need to be at the hospital for quite so long.'

'It seems strange without him.'

'It does, but he is happy with Becky. After all, he is her dog.'

'Dixon isn't my dog.'

Fiona stared, a slice of pizza half way to her mouth.

'What do you mean?'

'Technically he belongs to the Force.'

'Right,' Fiona said, not knowing what to say to that.

'When he retires I get first refusal but it means I probably won't be able to stay in the dog unit. It's difficult to mix a retired working dog with a working dog. They don't always get on so well.'

'That's a tough choice,' Fiona said.

'You know, I always thought it might be but after today it seems like it will be the easiest choice in the world.

'I mean, I know the Force would find him a loving home but the truth is I want him with me.'

'Could you walk away from work?'

'I always wondered but now I know.'

Tom looked so determined and sure that Fiona felt herself smile.

'Well, that's good,' she said and Tom nodded.

'Whatever happens I'm going to keep Dixon. If he can still work then great. If not, I'm going to give him the best retirement.'

They sat in silence for a little while. It was comfortable, just both of them lost to their own thoughts.

'Why don't we watch a movie and then get some sleep?' Fiona said.

'Sounds good.'

They were not half way through the

movie when Fiona knew that Tom was fast asleep. They had put the sofa bed up so they could stretch out their legs and had covered themselves with blankets to keep warm.

It had felt wonderfully cosy to Fiona and she enjoyed being able to snuggle up to Tom. She clicked the TV off and slipped quietly off the sofa bed, making sure Tom was well tucked in and headed off to her own room.

Fiona was awake early and padded into the kitchen area in search of a cup of tea. She put the kettle on as Tom stirred.

'What time is it?' he asked, running a hand through his hair and making it stick up at funny angles.

'Just before seven — sorry if I woke you.'

'It's good, I need to go home and get some clothes before I head back to the vet's.'

'You don't have to work?' Fiona asked and then put a hand over her mouth. He couldn't work as a dog handler without his dog, could he? 'I'm so sorry — that was a stupid thing to say.'

'It's fine,' Tom said, taking the offered mug of tea. 'Actually, I can still be on duty even if Dixon can't work but as it happens, we are at the start of four days off.'

'Well, I'll get showered and dressed and then I can come with you.'

'Are you sure?' Tom said although his face showed that he was grateful. 'I mean, I don't want to keep you from work.'

'You're not,' Fiona said with a smile. 'Even the self-employed get time off, you know.'

'Time off to spend with your friend,' Tom said, shaking his head.

'Exactly,' Fiona said, giving his arm a squeeze. 'Tom, seriously, there isn't anywhere else I would be right now. Becky completely understands that I need to be here.'

Tom looked at her for a long moment and then seemed to relax a little.

'I'll make it up to you, to both of you.'

'I'll hold you to that,' Fiona said and took herself off to the bathroom.

* * *

Tom's flat was very different from Fiona's. It was in a modern block, much closer to a Tube station. Tom had quickly showered and changed and then they were back out on the street and walking to the Underground.

'What?' Tom asked. 'I can see you want to ask me something.'

Fiona shrugged.

'Just that your flat doesn't seem very 'you'.'

'It's not but I had to move quickly and it was the only thing I could get.'

Fiona knew there was more to that story but didn't want to push things. Tom had too much on his mind with Dixon, to be getting into his history, which would no doubt bring up some of the stuff they had fallen out over.

Although Fiona was desperate to know why Tom had lied, today was not the day to ask such questions.

The vet's had just opened when they arrived and Sandy took them straight through to where Dixon was. As soon as he spotted Tom, Dixon was on his feet trying to get out of his cage.

'Steady there, boy,' Tom said and Dixon immediately went into a lopsided sit.

'Can I touch him?'

'Of course,' Sandy said. 'Are you all right to sit on the floor?'

Tom didn't answer, just sat himself down and took the blanket that Sandy offered him.

'It's important he stays as calm and still as possible — we don't want him pulling any of his stitches.'

Fiona knelt down beside Tom and Sandy carefully lifted Dixon on to Tom's lap, being careful of the IV line and his bandaged leg.

'Steady, boy,' Tom said softly. Dixon licked Tom's nose and then seemed content to settle down and be hugged.

'He looks good,' Fiona said quietly.

'He has had a good night,' Sandy said with a smile. 'If you're OK here I'll go find Tina who can give you a full update.'

Tom nodded, his eyes focused on Dixon.

'It's good to see you, Dixon. You scared me yesterday.'

Dixon whined a little and Tom scratched him in his favourite spot behind his ears. Fiona reached out a hand and Dixon licked it.

'Morning,' Tina, the vet from last night, said.

'Morning,' Fiona said as Tom seemed lost for words.

'He looks pretty bright this morning, considering.'

Tina nodded.

'He's certainly out of danger now.' She smiled at Tom who had finally dragged his eyes away from his beloved dog. 'His observations have been stable overnight which tells us that the internal bleeding has stopped and the operation yesterday was a success.'

Fiona could feel Tom relax a little beside her.

'What about his leg? I appreciate if it is too early to tell but . . . '

Tina nodded.

'I've sent Dixon's x-rays to a colleague of mine who specialises in trauma. I'm hoping that he will agree to take on Dixon's case. I've already spoken to the Force vet and he is in agreement that a specialist referral is appropriate.'

'Do you think he will be able to work again?' Tom asked.

Tina paused.

'I think it is unlikely, but that is not to say that Dixon won't have a full and happy life.'

Tom nodded.

'I'm actually kind of glad.'

Tina looked surprised but Fiona just smiled.

'I think Dixon has done his bit for Queen and country and I think it's time he enjoyed a safe and happy retirement.'

'Well I've made my recommendations to the Force vet and sent over all of Dixon's medical records and he is in agreement. He is expecting you to call later today to discuss what happens next.'

'Thanks, and thank you for everything you've done.'

'My pleasure,' Tina said. 'Spend some time with Dixon but he needs to rest so I would suggest another ten minutes and then maybe come back later this afternoon?'

'We will, thank you,' Fiona said as Tom buried his head in Dixon's fur.

Heart to Heart

As they stepped out of the vet's, Tom took Fiona's hand in his and they walked towards the Tube station together.

'Thank you for coming with me.'

'You don't need to thank me. I wouldn't want to be anywhere else.'

Tom squeezed her hand.

'Dixon looked good, considering,' Tom said.

'I can't believe how much better he looks and the vet was very upbeat. And you seem OK with him probably needing to retire,' Fiona added the last bit tentatively, not wanting to upset Tom.

'Do you know — I am. I've been thinking about it all night and I think maybe Dixon and I are both ready for a change.'

'Oh?' Fiona said, wondering exactly what Tom meant.

'Well, I've been thinking that maybe a career change would be good for me. I've been a police officer since I was nineteen.'

'Wow, that's a big decision.'

'Not really,' Tom said with a smile. 'I often wondered if the only reason I was staying was because I didn't want to leave Dixon.'

Fiona looked confused.

'Just because I want to leave doesn't mean Dixon gets to. If he can still work they would give him to another handler.'

'That's awful,' Fiona said. She couldn't imagine giving Archie to someone else. It had been hard enough leaving him with Becky, and Becky was his owner.

'It costs a lot to train working dogs and if I'm honest most of the dogs want to keep working.'

'I suppose,' Fiona said, not entirely convinced. 'What will you do?'

'I've always thought I would do dog training full time. You know, set up my own business properly?'

'Archie could be your poster boy!' Fiona said with a smile.

'Well, he was a challenge, wasn't he?'

'And look what you have done with him. He even comes back when I call . . . most of the time.'

Tom laughed.

'So you think I could do it then?'

'Definitely.'

'I think the dog training bit will be fine but the police doesn't really give you lots of experience in advertising or keeping the books,' he pointed out.

'That's easy,' Fiona reassured him. 'I can help you with that.'

'I can't ask you to do that, you have your own business to run.'

'You didn't ask, I offered. And besides, you were the guy who gave me free dog training lessons, remember? And I was a complete stranger back then.'

'You looked like you were in trouble,' Tom said with a shrug.

'Well, let me return the favour, now we are friends.'

They got to the Tube station and Tom stopped walking.

'Let's get some breakfast, I'm starving.'

There was a small café beside the station. Its windows were completely steamed up and the smells coming from the noisy interior made Fiona's stomach rumble and so she let herself be led inside.

It was nearly full of patrons and judging by the banter going back and forth they were mostly regulars. Tom found them a seat and they both ordered a full English.

'So I did a lot of thinking overnight,' Tom said as two plates loaded with bacon, eggs and the full works were placed in front of them.

'I can tell. That all sounds like life-changing stuff,' Fiona said with a smile.

'That wasn't the only thing I was thinking about,' Tom said seriously and Fiona had a feeling that they were about to get into what had happened between them.

'We don't have to talk about this now. We're OK and we can discuss that later when Dixon is better.'

'You said it yourself — Dixon is going to be fine and I need to talk about this, please?'

'OK,' Fiona said, giving him her full attention. She felt a knot of worry in the pit of her stomach, wondering what the explanation would be and how she would feel about it.

'My life is complicated,' Tom said before eating a mouthful of toast. Fiona nodded — that much she had figured out for herself.

'Firstly there is work, which is unpredictable and means that sometimes I have to cancel plans.'

Fiona nodded again. They had spoken about this and she had told him she understood. She knew he had more to say so she said nothing.

'Then there is my family.'

Fiona held her breath. He had never mentioned family before and she prepared herself for a bombshell.

'My brother died five years ago.'

'I'm so sorry,' Fiona said and reached out for his hand. Tom smiled at her gratefully.

'It's been really tough. But there's more.' He looked at her questioningly and she knew he was checking to see if she was ready to hear the rest.

'You can tell me anything, Tom, really,' she said, hoping that he wasn't about to break her heart but knowing that they both needed him to say what he had to say.

There could be no future for them if Tom didn't tell her about his life, however complicated it might be.

Tom shifted in his seat.

'My brother left behind his wife and son. Gina hasn't coped well with losing Pete and my nephew has some issues.'

Tom let out a held in breath.

'Jake is autistic. He's incredibly smart and a great kid but he doesn't cope well with the world.'

Tom looked at Fiona and Fiona tried to convey support and understanding in her expression alone. She knew that to interrupt Tom now would only make it harder for him to get through what he needed to say.

'He's eleven now and he can lash out when he gets upset, when his routine is upset or if the environment is too loud. The list of triggers is long.

'Gina doesn't cope well with him and so I often get called over to help. It can be any time, day or night.'

'Wow, that's a lot for you to cope with,' Fiona said. She couldn't imagine that kind of responsibility or how hard it could be.

'It is, and not everyone in my life can deal with it.' He looked at her searchingly now as if he were looking for the answer to a question.

'Is that why you didn't tell me?' Fiona asked, feeling both surprised and relieved at Tom's secret.

'Fiona, I've lost friends and more to my situation.' Tom clenched his hands into a fist.

'And that's OK because my family

come first but telling new people about it, well let's just say most of them smile and then that's it, I don't really see them again.'

'I'm sorry . . . ' Fiona started to say but Tom cut her off.

'You don't need to be sorry, believe me, I understand. It's a lot for any person to have to deal with a friend who might just not turn up and doesn't contact them for days. You've nothing to be sorry for.'

Tom smiled but Fiona could see the pain in his face.

'I think you misunderstand me,' Fiona said firmly. 'I'm sorry that you have all this to deal with and that your friends haven't been supportive of that.'

Tom stared at her and she looked evenly back at him.

'But that's not me. I stick with my friends through thick and thin.'

'I know you do that for Becky and I wasn't suggesting that you weren't a good friend but my life is complicated and messy, between Jake and my work, it makes me unreliable and sometimes a poor friend.'

'Tom, I need you to listen to me, really listen. What I am saying is that I understand all the demands on your time. I just wish you had told me sooner.'

'It's not so easy, you know? Hi, I'm Tom, I'm a police officer so I work crazy hours and can get called in at short notice, oh and by the way I have an autistic nephew who needs a lot of my time.'

'I'm not sure I would lead with that straight after 'hello',' Fiona said with a smile and Tom smiled back.

'I shouldn't have kept it from you, I was just scared that you would run a mile if you knew.'

Fiona smiled.

'Now I think it's my turn.'

Tom nodded, although he looked worried.

'I rang your phone and I'm guessing it was Gina that answered.'

Tom frowned and then realisation

seemed to strike him.

'Who did you think it was?' he asked quietly.

'I wasn't sure, but whoever it was seemed to know you and so when you said you had lost your phone, I, well, I got suspicious. Which I had no right to,' Fiona added hurriedly.

Tom shrugged.

'You would never have got suspicious if I told you the truth.'

'There's more I need to explain.'

Tom nodded.

'You can tell me anything,' he said.

Fiona sighed.

'I've had some bad experiences in the past.' Fiona could feel her voice wobble and fought to keep back the emotion that inevitably came any time she talked about Mark.

Tom squeezed her hand but said nothing, just gave her his full attention.

'I loved a guy called Mark and I thought he loved me too but he would keep secrets. Small at first but then they got bigger and when I would catch him out in a lie he would get angry and tell me that I was just paranoid. He said I was crazy.'

Fiona dug her fingernails into the palm of her free hand, as she tried to force away the memories that came with talking about Mark.

'For a while I thought he was right but then Becky caught him out and it turns out that he had been lying about a lot of things.'

Fiona sighed.

'And then I come along and keep things from you,' Tom said, shaking his head.

'You had every right to keep parts of your life to yourself,' Fiona said firmly. She wasn't telling him this to make him feel guilty, she just needed him to understand why she had done what she had.

'Becky told me that,' Fiona added softly, 'and she was right. I don't want to make you feel guilty, I just, I guess I need you to understand.'

Tom nodded.

'It was Becky that phoned, wasn't it?' Tom said, a ghost of a grin tugging at his lips.

'It was but she only did it for me. I was driving myself mad . . . ' Fiona trailed off, she wasn't sure that saying that would help the situation.

'I get it,' Tom said. 'It can be hard to trust again when you have been badly hurt by someone. I think we are quite alike, you and I.

'I didn't tell you the whole truth because I was afraid you wouldn't want to be around me but by doing that I made you feel like I was another Mark.' Tom raised an eyebrow in question and Fiona nodded.

'I'm sorry,' she said, that was all she could think of to say. She still couldn't believe her experience with Mark had nearly cost her a friend. A friend who she hoped could be so much more.

'I think we've both said that enough, don't you?' Tom asked and he was smiling now and Fiona could feel the sense of hopefulness in the air.

'I agree,' she said, smiling back.

'Well then, what do you say to putting all this mess behind us?'

'I'd like that,' Fiona said. She wanted to say that she wanted more than just friendship but now didn't seem like the time.

They had been through a lot and there was still Dixon to worry about. Friends for now seemed like the best option.

Together Again

Fiona sat beside Tom in the car they had hired to drive down to the specialist veterinary practice in Surrey. The miles seem to speed them towards their goal but at the same time the journey seemed to be taking for ever.

Fiona glanced across at Tom, who was focused on the road ahead and lost to his own thoughts. She didn't blame him. There had been a lot of change over the last couple of months.

Tom had decided that with Dixon retiring, it was time for him to leave the police service, too. It was a big decision and Fiona had been at his side throughout — not that she would want to be anywhere else.

'Penny for them?' Tom's voice cut through Fiona's thoughts and she jumped just a little. He reached a hand out to squeeze hers by way of apology for making her jump.

'Sorry,' Fiona said, smiling at him as he returned his hand to the steering wheel. 'I was just thinking about all that has changed recently.'

'It has been a bit of a whirlwind but I think I made the right decisions.'

'I know you did,' Fiona said confidently, 'and the business is starting to take off. Word is getting out there that you are the best in town.' Fiona giggled and Tom rolled his eyes.

'I still think you're wrong.'

'The fact that you have a load of female customers who make puppy-dog eyes at you, you mean?'

Tom frowned and shook his head. It was one of the things that Fiona had come to love about him, that he didn't see the fact that women found him so attractive.

There was no false modesty with Tom, she could see that in his face. He was genuinely bemused at the suggestion.

'Well, whatever it is, for a new starter

business you are doing great.'

'It's a relief, what with Dixon's vet bills.'

'Another good decision. As the vet said, he would do fine on three legs but if you can keep four then that would be better for him. I can't believe the police wouldn't pay for it.'

'They are a public service, remember? Not big business. They simply don't have that kind of money.'

Fiona nodded. She knew that Tom was right but it was still hard for her, thinking about all the work that Dixon had put in protecting the public.

'Twenty four thousand pounds to train a new Dixon, remember?' Tom said gently.

'I know, I know, but it just doesn't seem right that you have to come up with the money.'

'The retired police dog charity are paying half, Fi, I can't complain. And besides, Dixon is officially my dog now and I would do anything for him. I just hope he's doing OK.'

Now Fiona reached a hand across and squeezed Tom's.

'The vet said he's doing brilliantly. They wouldn't let him come home if he wasn't.'

'I just worry how I'm going to react to seeing him. I can't really imagine what he will look like.'

'He'll look like the superhero he is and he will have a full life ahead of him. The vet said it's an adjustment so don't be so hard on yourself.'

'I don't know how I would have got through all this without you,' Tom said softly.

'You would have done the same for me. In fact, you started all this by offering to help me with Archie.'

'Best decision I ever made,' Tom said, grinning at her. 'How is he?'

'Becky and Archie are coming down next weekend so you can see for yourself.' Fiona smiled at the thought. She had missed them both so much.

Even though she had spent a lot of time with Tom, it didn't mean she didn't miss her two other best friends.

'Dixon will be keen to see Archie again too, I think, and show off his leg.'

'And you'll finally get to meet Becky.'

'Let's hope she approves,' Tom said.

Fiona elbowed him gently.

'Of course she will.'

'You mean now she knows I'm not a liar or a love rat.'

Fiona rolled her eyes.

'I explained it all to her and she said we were as bad as each other, so I think she gets it.'

'We do make a right pair,' Tom said and Fiona felt her heart skip a beat at the words. She looked at Tom but he didn't seem to have realised what he had said and Fiona sighed.

'Don't worry we are nearly there,' Tom said, taking Fiona's sigh as a sign that she was impatient to get to Dixon, which she was, but that wasn't exactly what she was sighing about.

Later, she told herself, later when Dixon is home and settled, then it will be time to talk to Tom about how I feel.

They pulled into the car park and walked to the front door. Having checked in they were asked to take a seat.

Tom couldn't sit still and so Fiona moved closer to him and he slung his arm around her shoulders.

'It will be fine,' she whispered and he seemed to relax a little.

'Dixon's dad, please?' the vet called and Tom leapt to his feet and practically ran to the office, with Fiona close on his heels. The vet shook hands with both of them and asked them to take a seat.

'I'll just show you Dixon's x-rays and go through what you need to do for the next six weeks and then we can bring the boy in himself.'

Both Tom and Fiona were amazed at the x-rays which showed Dixon's new bionic leg.

'Can he run?' Tom asked.

'In six weeks when he is signed off, he can do whatever he likes but until the bone and skin heal, he needs to rest and be walked only on a lead.'

'Of course,' Tom said.

'Now I know he was a working dog and so boredom can be an issue.'

Tom laughed.

'Has he been up to mischief?'

The vet laughed, too.

'A little but my staff have been setting him puzzles with treats and that seems to keep him amused, for a little while at least.'

'We can do that for him at home,' Fiona said.

'Just don't let him overdo it. It would be a shame to come this far and then have a problem.'

'Don't worry, I'll make sure he rests,' Tom said.

'And when you're at work, he can stay with me,' Fiona said.

They had already discussed this. Tom needed to keep working and since Fiona could work from home, they had agreed that Tom would drop Dixon off at hers when he was dog training. Tom turned and smiled at her gratefully.

'Right, well I'll go and get Dixon. We'll meet you out the front. I don't want him to slip on the floor in here. Just pick up his meds from the front desk.'

Outside, with Fiona holding on to the plastic bag full of pain relief and antibiotics, Tom could not stand still. When Dixon's face appeared round the corner of the building, Tom started to move towards him. Dixon was straining on his lead and barking.

'Get down to his level,' the vet said but he didn't need to tell Tom. Tom had dropped to his knees and Dixon had jumped into his arms.

'Hi, buddy, I missed you,' Tom said and his voice wobbled with the emotion of the moment.

Fiona was desperate to hug Dixon, too, but knew that Tom needed this moment. Dixon rolled on to his back and waved his new bionic leg in Tom's face.

'Ah, yes, you'll need to be careful of that,' the vet said with a smile, 'it can pack quite a punch and Dixon hasn't quite figured that out yet.'

Tom inspected Dixon's new leg as Dixon barked.

'Well, Dixon seems impressed with it,' Tom said, smiling. 'Come and say hello, Fi.'

Fiona was by his side in an instant and Dixon leaned up and licked her nose as she stroked him.

'Dixon, you look amazing.' Fiona said, feeling the tears of relief come but not trying to stop them.

'Hey,' Tom said, nudging her, 'none of that or you'll have me going.'

'And me,' the vet said, holding out a hand to Tom. Tom stood up, clutching Dixon's lead, ignoring the hand and going in for a hug. The vet hugged back.

'Call if you are worried about anything and we'll see you in six weeks for what I hope is the final sign off.' The vet clapped Tom on the back and then went back to work.

Dixon was wiggling on the end of the

lead and so Tom picked him up and buried his face in his dog's fur.

'Dixon, if it's possible you look better than ever, bud. You are going to turn heads at the park.'

Dixon whined as if to say that he knew that and could they just get off home.

'I know that noise,' Tom said, laughing. 'Home?' Dixon licked Tom on the nose.

Tom opened the back door and laid Dixon on his dog bed, which he had brought with them. He slipped Dixon into his harness and attached him to the seat belt for safety.

'Why don't you sit in the back with Dixon, and I'll drive,' Fiona said.

'Do you mind?' Tom said but his face told Fiona that her suggestion had been a good one.

'Of course not! You haven't seen Dixon for three weeks and I think you guys need some time together.'

Tom shut the door on Dixon's side and practically ran round the other side before climbing in. Dixon shifted himself so that he could lay his head on Tom's lap. Fiona got into the driver's seat, took one look in the rear view mirror, smiled and drove off.

Not Before Time!

Dixon was fast asleep on Fiona's sofa and Fiona was hard at work when the doorbell rang. She finished typing her sentence and then went to press the buzzer that would open the front door.

Dixon had finally been signed off as completely fit the week before but Tom had continued to drop him off when he was training puppies. He said that despite Dixon's exemplary behaviour, he was a distraction to the much younger dogs.

Fiona opened the front door and Tom walked in.

'What happened to you?' Fiona said, biting her lip to keep the smile off of her face.

'Rosie happened to me,' Tom said trying to pretend to be cross but failing miserably. He was covered in mud from the knees down.

'It makes me feel kind of better about Archie knowing that other dogs get you into trouble too.'

'Rosie decided that she was going to go for a wallow, in that muddy bit of pond.'

'Ah,' Fiona said, grabbing a towel from the cupboard and handing it to him. 'Time for emergency jogging bottoms?' she asked.

'I think so,' Tom said ruefully as he took off his shoes.

Fiona grabbed the trousers from her cupboard. She had suggested that Tom leave some clothes at hers, the last time Rosie had pulled Tom into the lake. Rosie was a St Bernard, still a puppy but when she put her mind to something there was no stopping her.

Tom took the trousers and the towel and headed for the small bathroom. Dixon looked up from his nap but seemed content to wait to greet Tom when he was less muddy.

Fiona busied herself with making hot chocolate and finding the cookies she had brought from the bakery earlier in the day as a treat.

There had been so many times since Dixon had been signed off that she had nearly brought up the topic of her feelings for Tom but each time, it just hadn't felt right and so Fiona had pushed them away.

She was beginning to wonder if she would ever find the courage — as was Becky who was threatening to tell Tom herself, how Fiona felt.

'I was wondering if we could have a chat.' Tom's words cut through Fiona's thoughts but she wasn't entirely sure what he had actually said. Fiona thought it might be her imagination but Tom looked a little unsettled.

'OK,' Fiona said, feeling a stab of worry. Maybe Tom had decided to move out of the city? It was something he had mentioned in passing.

She gave herself a few moments to compose herself before joining Tom on the small sofa. Tom had Dixon on his lap and he was hugging him close.

Fiona waited but Tom didn't seem to want to say anything now. Fiona now felt desperate to say something, maybe to get in her feelings before Tom could tell her he was leaving.

'Tom, I . . . ' she started to say but Tom cut her off.

'Would you mind if I said what I've been thinking about first? I've been trying to say this for an age . . . '

'OK,' Fiona managed to say. Now she knew for sure. He hadn't wanted to tell her that he was leaving London.

Maybe he was worried how she would react and so she forced her face into a neutral expression and reminded herself that being a good friend, meant supporting them, however painful it might be for her personally.

'Go ahead,' Fiona said cautiously.

'It's been crazy the last few months, I know,' Tom said. He was talking slowly as if he were having to pick each word with care. Fiona nodded, that was certainly true.

Tom seemed to have stopped and

Fiona felt like he would never get to the point.

'Look, if you are trying to tell me that you want to move out of London, you don't really need to, I've kind of guessed. I'll miss you and Dixon but I support your decision.' Fiona spoke so quickly that it felt like her words had all joined together. With Tom staring at her, she was sure that she would need to repeat herself.

She opened her mouth but closed it again when Tom started to shake his head and laugh. Fiona didn't think Tom leaving was much to laugh about but she held her tongue.

'Fi, did you really think that was what I wanted to talk to you about?'

Now it was Fiona's turn to stare.

'I don't know,' she said a little crossly and Tom stopped laughing.

'You're right, sorry. It's wrong for me to expect you to read my mind.' He took a deep breath.

'What I've have been trying to say for weeks is that I love you, Fiona. I think I have since the moment I first saw you. I don't know how you feel and so I don't want to put you under any pre . . . '

Fiona silenced him with a kiss. A kiss that was both gentle and passionate.

'I love you, too,' Fiona said, pulling away slightly. 'I've been trying to tell you but I wasn't sure how you felt, either.'

Tom chuckled.

'I imagine Becky is going to call us all kinds of idiots.'

'She already has,' Fiona said smiling back and looking into Tom's eyes.

'I'm sorry I made everything so complicated,' he said, pulling Fiona into his arms.

'You didn't do that all by yourself,' she pointed out.

'What are we like?'

'Well the most important thing,' Fiona said, pulling Tom's arms around her, 'is that we got there in the end.'

'Thank goodness,' Tom said, kissing Fiona on the top of her head. 'I feel like you are my missing half,' he said softly.

'Mine, too.'

They stayed holding each other tight for some time, content in their closeness.

'Why did you think I would want to move out of London?'

'Well, you mentioned it a few times and when you said you didn't know how to tell me something, well I figured that was it.'

Tom's chuckle rumbled in his chest.

'We need to get better at saying how we feel,' he said.

'I don't think we'll have a problem now,' Fiona said before reaching up for a kiss.

'I would love to move one day, though.' Tom said.

'Me, too,' Fiona said, 'but what about Jake?'

'I hope that I could persuade Gina to come too. I think Jake would do much better out of the city.

'We could find a place with a good school for him that meets his needs, and we could find a place for them to live that wasn't too far away from us. If that's all right by you?'

Fiona shifted in his arms so that she could see his face and so that he could see hers.

'It's one of the things that I love about you, Tom. Your love of your family and commitment to them. I want to be a part of that too. And I think the idea is perfect.'

'Jake takes a long time to warm to people, to trust them, but I already see him responding to you. I knew you were special but that clinched it.'

Now Fiona laughed.

'You were right, he's a great kid.'

'Not everyone sees that.'

'That's their loss.'

Tom kissed her once more and all thoughts of anything else left their minds.

Happy Tears

'Becky, really why are you in such a hurry today?' Fiona grumbled as, for the hundredth time that day, Becky told her to get a move on.

'We are going to be late,' Becky said, tapping her foot on the ground.

'For a dog walk,' Fiona said, slowly rolling her eyes, 'and we have ten minutes yet, that's plenty of time to get to the park.' Fiona searched under the sofa and found her missing shoe, no doubt left there by Archie, who had been in a mischievous mood all day.

'And I'm sure Tom and Dixon won't leave just because we are a few minutes late.' Fiona didn't have the chance to say anything else as Becky threw her coat at her and it hit her full in the face.

'OK, fine,' Fiona said, pulling it on.

It had been great to finally have Becky back in London. She had managed to find a place to stay within walking distance and Fiona thought her life was pretty perfect, except when her friend got into one of the moods she was in today. Becky had been fidgety since she arrived, telling Fiona to stop work early and chill out with her.

Fiona shook her head. Whatever had got into her friend, she hoped a long walk in the park would cure her of it. And seeing Tom was never a bad thing, she told herself with a grin.

'Come on, you,' Becky said one last time, rolling her eyes. Fiona grabbed her phone, shoved it in her pocket and followed Becky out of the front door.

They hurried into the park and headed towards the lake. Archie was so well behaved now that they let him off the lead. Archie trotted a little way in front of them with his nose in the air.

Both Becky and Fiona laughed when he turned around and barked at them. This seemed to be his way of asking if it was OK to run ahead. Becky made shooing motions and Archie ran off, his tail wagging, which meant he had caught Dixon's scent and was running off to greet him first.

'Tom really is a miracle worker,' Becky said, watching her dog. 'I never could get Archie to do anything, despite all the classes.'

'He has a gift,' Fiona said a little dreamily.

'I don't think you ever have thanked me for lending you my dog so that you could meet the man of your dreams.'

Fiona laughed. She had in fact thanked Becky many times, as had Tom, for that matter. Fiona looked ahead and she could now see that Archie was sitting by Tom's side, waiting for them patiently. Tom waved and Fiona waved back.

Now it was Fiona's turn to pick up the pace. As she walked towards Tom she realised that Dixon was sitting behind him. Her fast walk turned into a jog.

'Is Dixon all right?' she asked a little breathlessly as she reached Tom's side.

'He's fine, Fi, but he does have something he wants to ask you.'

Fiona looked down as Dixon walked around to sit in front of Tom. It was then that Fiona realised that Dixon was wearing a sign around his neck.

'Fiona, will you marry my dad?' it said. And underneath it read: 'And be my mum?'

Fiona stared at the sign, wondering if she was dreaming.

'Well, don't keep the poor chap waiting,' Becky said and Fiona wasn't sure if she meant Tom or Dixon.

Tom was now down on one knee beside Dixon and in his hand he held out a box containing ring. A ring with diamonds.

'I love you, Fi. Will you make me the happiest man on the planet and be my wife?'

Fiona had her hands over her mouth to try to catch the sob but she moved them away as she knew it was time for her to answer.

'Yes,' she said. 'Yes, of course.'

Tom pushed the delicate diamond ring on to her finger and then pulled her into his arms and thoroughly kissed her.

Dixon and Archie were barking and running around them in circles but Becky had disappeared.

'There is one more thing,' Tom said, finally putting Fiona down. Fiona couldn't imagine anything that could make this moment more perfect.

'I've got you an engagement present,' Tom said, turning her around. Fiona could see Becky walking towards her with a bundle of something in her arms.

'You've talked about it so much and since we are getting married I figured we could expand our family.'

Fiona could feel the tears come and this time she didn't bother to fight them as Tom lifted a small black puppy from Becky's arms.

Fiona buried her face in the puppy's fur and kissed her. The puppy tentatively licked her nose and then started to wiggle so Tom handed her over to Fiona.

'She is Dixon's half-sister — they have the same mum.'

'She's gorgeous,' Fiona managed to say, laughing now as the puppy licked at her happy tears.

Dixon was whining, clearly wanting to meet the new arrival and so Fiona knelt down and Dixon gently sniffed his new sister, giving his seal of approval. Archie trotted over and did the same. Tom was soon on his knees beside Fiona, stroking the puppy's soft head.

'I love you,' Fiona said leaning over to kiss Tom.

'I love you, too,' Tom said.

'And I love you both,' Becky said, not bothering to hide the fact that she was crying too.

They all stood up each with a dog in their arms and did a sort of funny group hug.

'Archie wants to know if he can be best man,' Becky said and Archie barked.

'Of course,' Tom said, 'he and Dixon are the reason we met.'

They all laughed before Tom pulled Fiona into his arms, being mindful of the newest member of the family and kissed her.

'I think it's time for a photo to commemorate this moment,' Becky said. She walked up to a young couple and said something before handing over her phone.

'Right, dogs front and centre,' Becky said. Dixon and Archie sat down in the front row. Tom had his arm around Fiona, who held her new puppy in her arms and Becky linked her arm through Fiona's. It was the perfect family photo.

We do hope that you have enjoyed reading this large print book.

Did you know that all of our titles are available for purchase?

We publish a wide range of high quality large print books including:
Romances, Mysteries, Classics
General Fiction
Non Fiction and Westerns

Special interest titles available in large print are:
The Little Oxford Dictionary
Music Book, Song Book
Hymn Book, Service Book

Also available from us courtesy of Oxford University Press:
Young Readers' Dictionary
(large print edition)
Young Readers' Thesaurus
(large print edition)

For further information or a free brochure, please contact us at:
Ulverscroft Large Print Books Ltd.,
The Green, Bradgate Road, Anstey,
Leicester, LE7 7FU, England.
Tel: (00 44) **0116 236 4325**
Fax: (00 44) **0116 234 0205**

Other titles in the
Linford Romance Library:

THE CHRISTMAS VISITOR

Jill Barry

Rich man's daughter Eleanor is horrified when her father invites disgraced nobleman Rupert to join the family Christmas house party. But when the pair meet by accident, she finds him attractive, then is dismayed to learn his identity. Rupert and his valet fit in well, while gentle scheming by the indispensable Mr Steadman enhances Eleanor and Rupert's dawning relationship. Upstairs and downstairs, romance blossoms — but can both his lordship and his valet make amends for their past mistakes?

SWAN PRINCESS

Penny Oates

Talented young ballerina Gina is struggling following the death of her mother, the failure of her choreographer father's new ballet, and the desertion of her fiancé David. Trying to support her grieving father and save the ballet company her parents set up, she is outraged when rich, brooding businessman Jude Alexander criticises her approach and offers to become a partner. His money could solve all their problems — but she suspects his motives, and vows to fight him tooth and nail . . .

FINDING PRINCE CHARMING

Victoria Garland

After a disastrous first night, Eleanor abandons London's West End for her grandparents' home in the Scottish Highlands. But her plans to lie low are foiled when she's asked to save the village panto. With an old flame waiting in the wings, some real-life Ugly Sisters making mischief, and a Hollywood star setting her pulse racing, Eleanor finds more than she bargained for in not-so-sleepy Tullymuir. Will she also find her Prince Charming and get the happy ending she deserves?

DEAD RINGER

Sarah Swatridge

When Lizzie Holden drives a wagon into the town of Jacob's Creek, Connor Riordan is smitten. Though she is betrothed to Jeremiah Newham, Lizzie slowly begins to realise her fiancé is not all he seems. And her arrival has inspired disquiet amongst the townsfolk. For Lizzie bears a striking resemblance to Elizabeth King, a young woman who turned down a rich suitor to marry one of her father's ranch hands — and perished when her homestead was burned to the ground . . .

WITH ALL MY HEART

Dawn Knox

Germany, 1938. Anti-Jewish feeling is increasing and when Miriam and Rebekah's parents are killed in a bomb attack, the girls are snatched from their lives of wealth and privilege to be abandoned in an orphanage. There, the sisters meet fellow Jew, Karl, and the three young people are assisted out of Germany on the Kindertransport train. Miriam and Karl feel a connection but circumstances part them before they reach England. How can they possibly find each other again?